A DEBT FOR LOVE

Line/Copy editing by Emma
Cover design and formatting by Rotoscope Design

Foreword

This story is not a light romance, please check the content warning list at the end of the book or find it on my Instagram (@michelle_eveleen) before you decide to keep reading. The MMC is not a good guy, nor will he ever be one.

- There is only one way to find redemption for those that bring darkness; from those who seek it.

*For all the good girls that don't just crave the darkness, they **need** it.*
Welcome home.

PROLOGUE

ISOBEL

Grief and love.

Two feelings I never knew could coexist together, could grow together, could morph together until I could no longer tell the difference.

I knew pain and love thrived together. I had experienced that on some level too, but the pain that was to come would be different. It would be enjoyable, addicting, something I didn't know how to escape, or want to.

I would fall straight into hell and wonder if the fire is where I was always meant to be. And even though I was in hell, I would feel heaven in ways I never thought possible.

I would feel the fluffy caressing of clouds whilst the burning etched at parts of my skin, branding and suffocating me.

The devil was not who I expected, but I would end up worshiping him, nonetheless.

CHAPTER ONE

ISOBEL

The cool autumn air brushes against my face as I wrap my cream scarf around another layer. The flight from Chicago was a smooth one, and I knew that I should just rest this first night and start my investigating tomorrow; but I couldn't. I had tried to lie down, tried to watch American Horror Story, my go to comfort show, but it felt like bugs were crawling over my skin.

I couldn't wait another day, and I didn't want to. My entire purpose for being here was to find answers, so I had put on my tights, a pencil skirt with a knit top and my favourite boots that fell just below my knees, before messaging my driver Lewis to meet me downstairs. I had bought Lewis with me from Chicago and he had hired a cream-coloured Volvo for our time in Devils Lake. I had been to North Dakota before, but never to this town. It felt very small compared to my home, with more open land and a breathtaking lake that is enclosed with pine trees and cliffs. I couldn't work out why my father was here, though; he had never mentioned it before, but he had always been unpredictable.

We pull up to the last known location my father was; The Northern Pike Bar.

Why were you here?

I look out from my window, noticing mainly old trucks parked outside, I can already tell that I won't fit in at this kind of place, and really, I shouldn't even be here at all, my mother would kill me if she found out what I was doing; but I could no longer do nothing. The police had said the leads for my father's disappearance had gone cold, and although they said they would still be investigating, part of me felt like they didn't really care, maybe it had something to do with the fact that my father is Native American, or maybe because he had found himself having a few run-ins with the police over the years. Either way, the not knowing was eating at my mind, causing a blockage with everything else I wanted to be doing. The where, why, and what would continuously circle around my brain until I felt like ripping at my skull.

My parents divorced when I was five, and seventeen years later they never really wanted much to do with each other, besides when it involved me. But Mum grew tired of Dad's impulsiveness, his unpredictable behaviour, traits I think she loved before becoming a parent, but she grew up and my father never did. I pull my mirror out of my Louis Vuitton bag, taking in my features quickly, making sure my lip-gloss and mascara are where they were meant to be. I inherited my dad's big, dark eyes, his dark hair and skin, but the rest of my features are from my white mother.

"You sure you want to do this?" Lewis asks, causing me to jump slightly.

"It will probably all be pointless, but at least I can say I did something. Even if I just try, maybe my mind will clear away for me to stop thinking about it," I sigh, looking back out at the wooden bar.

My phone dings and I pull it out to read the message,

Bre
Cocktails?

I sigh again. I also hadn't told my best friend what I was doing either.

Spending the weekend with Mum xx

God, I was surely going to hell for lying to her, but if she knew what I was doing, she would have insisted on coming, Bre would never take no for an answer when it came to me, and this is something I wanted to do alone.

"Do you want me to come in?"

"No, thank you Lewis," I open the door and hop out of the car, the fresh night air hitting me once more, making me want to get straight back in and drive back to The Lodge where my wood heater is waiting.

Dad's last bank transaction was from this bar at 9:37pm, and I needed to at least see it, see the place he wanted to be, maybe try to understand why he had strayed so far from home. Montana is where I grew up, where I lived for most of my life, but once I moved to Chicago, Mum came with me, wanting to leave the town just as much as me and start somewhere fresh. Dad however, stayed and although I still saw him occasionally, it grew less and less the older I got, and once I moved; it became Christmas and my birthday, but eventually it dropped back to just Christmas.

I open the creaking door, and I am immediately hit with warmth, stale beer, and cigarettes. There are a couple pool tables, a small stage with live music, the bar, and to the left is an entrance to a dining room. The best part of the whole place is the open fireplace flickering in the corner.

"What's your name, sweetheart?" My view of the fire is interrupted by a tall man who looks to be in his early thirties. He isn't ugly, but he also wasn't my type; not that I have a type anymore.

I clear my throat. "Isobel," I reach into my bag to pull out my phone, and as I look up to him, he is smirking. "Have you seen this man before?" I show him a picture of my dad, and his smirk disappears. I guess he was expecting me to get my phone out for other reasons.

"No, but how about I buy you a drink?" His lazy grin returns before he takes a slow sip of his beer, his eyes never leaving mine.

"No, thank you." I walk past him to ask the next person, but accidentally bump into a girl carrying two drinks.

"Watch it!" She turns to face me angrily.

"Sor-" I begin to apologise before she cuts me off.

"What in the fuck are you doing in here?" Her eyes moving up and down my overly dressed attire. "You don't belong here," she says with spite. The nerves creeping into my skin, making their way straight for my heart.

Maybe this wasn't a good idea.

CHAPTER TWO

ISOBEL

I place my dread down inside me. "Have you seen this man?" The girls eyes form into slits as she looks at the photo.

"No, and if I were you, I would leave. The men in here won't hesitate to ignore the word no, and the girls are meaner than me. Pretty rich girl like you is just asking to get her hair ripped out," she walks away from me without a second glance.

I rub at my eyes. Maybe I should have dressed in jeans and a flannel shirt. I head to the bathroom, needing to distance myself from the unwanted glances. I run the cold-water tap, leaning down to cup some in my hand and splash to the back of my neck. I stare up at my reflection, wondering if there were any answers hiding in the mirror. Why the hell my father decided to be here is a mystery. There was a time when being around these kinds of people felt less intimidating, but that feels like a lifetime ago now.

The creak of the heavy door squeaks as three women around my age walk in. One immediately looks at me in disgust as the other two slowly approach. I keep my stare blank, but swallow at my dry throat.

"Look at that bag Jessie," Jessie, who has bright red hair and a crooked smile, whistles.

"That's some fancy rich shit right there." The three of them back me into the corner of the wall as I inconspicuously slide my phone into the back of my skirt.

"I'm not here to cause any trouble," I keep the fear from my eyes even if my hands tremble slightly.

The first girl, with a face that looks like she was squished against a wall, laughs at me. "Girls looking like you only come here for trouble. Bored of your easy life?" She tilts her head and I fight the rage simmering in my hands; no longer do they shake from fear. Three of them against me, even if I swing first, I would not stand a chance, and although I would definitely enjoy the look of shock on their faces when I landed a solid punch, one that would squish her stupid face in even further; it will end my investigation for the night.

"What do you want?" I whisper, again not from fear, but if they think I am scared, it might make them go easier on me.

"The bag and the watch," the third girl says quietly, almost like she doesn't actually want to be a part of this.

I hand them over, trying to keep the glare from my eyes as I do. There is nothing in my bag besides some lip-gloss and a brush. Everything else I need is on my phone. The bag that is easily replaceable is not worth getting beaten to a pulp over, but something about going down without a fight grinds at me.

I am not being weak; I am being smart.

They leave in laughter, like the stupid bitches are the funniest people to walk this earth. Maybe I should find out which one of these shitty pickup trucks belong to them and cut the breaks. See how goddamn funny that would be. I smile to myself as I envision them crashing, only for me to come back along and grab my unscathed bag.

The only way for me to stop my anger is to picture something horrible happening to the person who caused it. The level of anger will depend on how badly I punish them in my mind.

I decide to eat here, having a steak that is overcooked but not inedible, with a red wine. I wonder if my father ate here, if he had a beer at the bar, or maybe played a round of pool? But with who and why? Surely most of the people that come here are regulars, some probably even eat here every night. Someone has to have seen him; someone has to know something.

I down the rest of my wine and begin making the rounds around the growingly rowdy people. There is a fight that breaks out while I am showing one guy the picture of my father, before he shoves me aside to rush amongst the fighting.

I exhale before stomping over to the next guy. He has a cap on with brown strands of hair that peak out, and bloodshot eyes that smile as I approach. "Have you seen this man before?" I ask without even saying hello. He studies the picture before clicking the side of his mouth as his right eye winks shut. "For the right price, I will tell you."

Feeling completely defeated with this night, if I had the cash, I would hand it over even if he knows nothing. "I have no money on me," I reply sharply.

"There are other forms of payment. That pretty mouth of yours would look great around my dick," he smirks.

I resist the urge to gag. "This pretty mouth also comes with teeth," I sneer before heading to the bar, well and truly ready to give up.

I slide on the barstool, placing my phone down and resting my face in my hands, the bartender approaching me immediately. "Whiskey," I say before he can ask.

"What kind?" His eyes holding less kindness with my abruptness.

"Any."

I pay using my phone and he slides the glass in front of me. I take in the guy's hands sitting beside me. A large scar is on his right hand that cups his beer. I risk a glance further up and notice he is sitting alone, the impressive muscle in his arm tensing as he brings the beer to his mouth, taking a long sip. His dark blonde hair is pushed back, but one strand has fallen just to his eye level. His skin that looks like he works outside is covered in patch work black tattoos. I find my body heating quickly, like his presence is too intense to be around. I quickly down my whiskey, hoping it will give me a small bit of courage.

I clear my throat and pull up my phone, "excuse me, I'm just wondering-"

"Fuck off."

I suck in a gasp, shock flickering across my face. "It- it will only take a second of your time," I stumble.

He turns to face me, and my eyes flick to his, their green shade finding my own dark. There is something hard behind his gaze, something cold and almost lifeless. "Fuck. Off." He says with no emotion at all, and I find myself fumbling from the barstool and leaving without a glance back.

CHAPTER THREE

ISOBEL

With a scolding hot shower and my lavender skincare done, I still struggle to sleep. Even though the bed is snuggly and the pillows as comfortable as my own, I toss and turn. Long erased from my memory are the three girls, no they have been replaced by something much more consuming.

Green, lifeless eyes.

In the moment I felt nothing but shock, but as the hours ticked away, the anger creeped in. Anger that he felt like he could be so rude, so blunt, without even giving me the time to talk. And every time I attempted to punish him with my mind, his lifeless eyes welcomed it. It frightened me and angered me further, my usual technique to diminish the emotion being smothered by the eerie feeling that he would fear nothing, that every punishment would be enjoyable.

I give up, aggressively pushing the blankets away from my body and reaching for the bedside light, my blue light glasses, and my laptop. If I am going to be awake, I may as well be productive.

At some point I fall to sleep. I wake to the sounds of vibration, my laptop open beside me, and my neck sore from sleeping with two pillows. The light is filtering in from the sides of the curtain as I tiredly rub at the sleep in my eyes. The vibration continues and I quickly shoot out my hand, reaching for my phone.

"Hello?" I answer without even looking at who called me.

"Isobel? Were you still sleeping?" Mum asks.

"Uhh yeah," I answer honestly. I put her on loudspeaker and check the time. 11:15.

"Did you go out with Bre last night?"

"No, just a late-night writing."

"You're writing again?" Mum fails to hide the excitement in her tone.

"I'm trying to. How are you going?" I attempt to steer the conversation away from me.

"Oh, I am fine darling, was going to bring a coffee and our favourite cake over."

Shit.

"I can't today Mum, I am heading out with Bre." I was surely going to hell from all this lying.

"Oh, maybe tomorrow then?" I can hear the hurt in her tone and the guilt rises in my stomach.

"I will let you know; my agent messaged me about having a meeting." I cringe at the weak attempt to avoid my mother.

"Alright darling, well I love you and we will catch up soon. Have a lovely day with Bre."

"I love you too Mum," hanging up, I flop back into bed.

At some point, I am going to have to tell them both where I am.

I find a small coffee shop with hanging plants and wooden furniture where I have a late breakfast that turns into lunch. Going over everything from last night, avoiding the green eyes, I reevaluate everyone's face as they looked at the picture of my father. Trying to remember if anyone showed any recognition as they looked, but nobody showed any flicker of emotion. The women I asked being not helpful at all, but once the men realised I wasn't interested in getting to know them, they turned out to be more useless.

One more night.

I will give it one more night of trying, hoping for new people before I go home. At least I can say I tried something, that I didn't just give up on him. I walk around for a while before heading back to The Lodge to change for tonight. I opt for simpler clothes this time, some dark pants, a plain top, and a thick coat.

The atmosphere in the bar is the same as the night before, with some new faces and plenty of familiar ones as well. My eyes are instantly drawn to the bar, to the eyes that stared at me with nothing behind them. He is sitting in the same spot he was last night, and I inhale a shaky breath as I avoid him completely. Then I continue to avoid every face I talked to last night. Luckily, the three girls that stole my bag are nowhere to be seen. Maybe they really did crash on the way home. I try not to smile at the thought.

After a fish dinner and more faces that either light up with my approach or turn their nose down at me, I feel exhausted. Exhausted from talking to people that I don't want to, exhausted from the travel and sleepless night, exhausted from the confusion, and exhausted from missing someone that has been missing from my life for much longer than his disappearance.

My phone begins vibrating against my leg, and I reach into my bag to pull it out. Bre is ringing, "shit," I breathe. I quickly duck out the back door before answering, not wanting Bre to hear all the noise from the bar. The cold night air brushes against my skin, and I pull my coat tighter around myself. There isn't much lighting back here, but it is silent and empty.

"Hey!" I answer excitedly.

"Don't you hey me Iz," she says flatly.

"Is everything okay?"

"I happened to bump into your mum."

Well, there goes keeping them out of my business. "Bre-"

"And I found it interesting that she asked how our day went together," she says with attitude.

"What did you say?" I ask nervously.

"Well, I obviously covered for you, but you have some explaining to do."

I sigh, "I'm at Devils Lake."

"Iz-"

"You don't need to worry because I will be coming home tomorrow. I just needed to do something, you know?"

"I understand, but I would have come with you. We could have had a little girl's weekend," her tone has already changed from angry to concerned.

"It's just something I needed to do on my own, but it has been a waste of time, so I will be home tomorrow, okay?"

"Okay, I will come see you tomorrow night, safe travels Iz."

"Thanks Bre," I hang up as the back door opens. I had walked five metres around the corner as I paced while talking. Feeling the cold more than ever, I keep my head down as I head back for the door.

"Look who it is," I look up to find three men smiling at me. Not a comforting smile, a predatory one. The one that smirks the hardest is the one I threatened with my teeth the night before. I look behind me to emptiness, and in front is the bar, but I would never make it through them to safety. My body begins to shake, not from the cold this time.

"I can give you money," I attempt at trying to spare myself a lifetime of despair.

They laugh at me, "you think we are out here for money? Oh no sweetheart, we came to see what's under that coat." These men are the kind that would enjoy hunting innocent animals that can never fight back. They spend their lives going after targets that will never pose a threat to them. I back away a little as the three of them close in on me, and I realise as my bottom lip begins to tremble that no amount of punishment in my mind will ease the pain that they will put me through.

I had already lost such a massive part of myself before, the part that had me enjoying the look and touch from a man, the part of me that felt innocent even if I wasn't, because my idea of innocence was so distorted. But if these three take me right here,

I know I will fight, and I know it will never be enough, and any chance I have of holding onto myself will be lost forever. I know it deep in my bones that this is something I will never recover from.

"Please," I beg, the tears stinging the edges of my eyes with the cold breeze.

"I want to hear you beg the entire time," the guy caresses my cheek in an oddly gentle gesture. Like he isn't about to force himself and his two friends onto me. Then he rips my body close to his as the other two approach, all of them digging their fingers into my clothes as I thrash and scream. Kicking at anybody part I can, and using my lungs as loud as they will go, but my pleas are drowned out from the band playing inside and even if they were heard, no one here would come to save me.

I beg for nothing more than darkness now.

CHAPTER FOUR

ISOBEL

My coat and bag have been discarded, my shirt ripped in different places, as the two of them have me pinned to the ground. The smirking asshole is unbuttoning my pants, and I smash my head against the ground. Please, please take me darkness. "Stop her!" He orders, noticing me trying to knock myself out. One hand swoops in to stop my head hitting the ground. "We wouldn't want you to miss this," he smiles as he continues to tug at my pants, the bile forcing its way up my throat.

I force my body and mind into a calm place, into a numbness that won't give any of these guys a flicker of emotion, give them the satisfaction of my tears or screams. I would not beg now, and I would not cry. The tears will come later and they probably would never end. Remaining unfeeling is the only fight I can give them. They want every pained reaction from me. They want me to scream until my vocal cords break, but I will not give over that part of myself also.

"Accepting your fate, sweetheart?" He smirks down at me and I force my eyes to meet his, force the deadness to settle into me and him, and for a moment he hesitates. Maybe he won't be able to do this without me screaming. He roughly grabs my mouth, "I don't need this pretty thing to be screaming to fuck you, sweetheart." The vomit burns my throat, but I push it down and keep my stare dead.

I will not give him what he wants. I will not give in.

Before he has time to pull my pants further down, there is a gasp beside me, and then the right side of my body is free. Without even having the time to react, the guy on my left receives two quick jabs to his face before his arm is swiftly snapped backwards. His screams fill the empty night as the one by my pants starts backing away. I fight through the shock as I rip my pants back up and scurry for my coat to wrap around myself.

I should run, call for Lewis to pick me up immediately and not stop driving until we reach Chicago, but I don't. I am mesmerised by the muscles on his back as he corners the last guy. Taking his time, I realise the hunters have become the hunted. The back of his dark blonde hair and his mismatched tattoos cause my heart rate to pick right back up. Him. Out of everyone in the bar, I never pictured that the green eyes would be the ones to save me.

You begged for the darkness to take you.

Is he the darkness I called out for?

Close by, one of them is completely still on the ground, and the other is groaning and clutching his arm close to his chest.

"Atlas-" the third guy begs. "W- we didn't know she was your girl," he holds up his hands in defeat.

Quicker than I have ever seen somebody move, Atlas smashes his fist with three jabs to different parts of his face. The guy's head smashing back and hitting the wall of the bar, then Atlas is twirling something in his hands. I strain my eyes to see the knife moving with ease between each finger. My breath hitches with anticipation. "If she was my girl, you would all be dead," then he grabs his hand and in one swift movement jams the knife through the middle of his hand, I can see the tip well and truly poking out through the bottom of his palm. He screams out in agony, "you scream louder than she ever would have for you," Atlas's tone is mocking. The shock moves out of my body as I realise it is replaced by something new; excitement. I must have hit my head harder than I realise against the ground to feel this way, but here it is; the man giving out my punishment inside my head.

"Please...it- it won't happen again," the man is crying and I smile, I smile that I controlled my own tears while he could not. Pathetic.

Atlas slaps the side of his face, and the guy flinches away with fear. "No, it won't," he says simply. "I'll be needing that back though."

The guy holding his wrist looks at Atlas with confusion before the knife is ripped free from his hand and his screams fill the cold night once more.

Atlas wipes the blade against the guy's jumper before beginning to head away. He offers me one quick glance before walking past me. I scramble to my feet, keeping the coat wrapped tightly around myself. "Wait-" I call out. He continues his walking for the carpark around the corner. "Please," I call again. He turns to face me, offering no words of comfort. He simply stares at me. "Th-thank you," I stumble on my words. Maybe the shock was creeping back in.

He shrugs, but still offers me no words. "How did you do that?" Is the only thing I can think of to say.

"Hurting people comes easy to me," he says without a flicker of emotion.

His words should frighten me, should terrify me more than the other three, the feeling that this man in front of me is easily way more dangerous, but I don't feel fear with his words, I feel that tiny ember of excitement at the pit of my stomach; begging for me to let it grow. "You saved me," I say simply, even though it was anything but simple what he did. He offers me no reasons of why, just continues to stare at me, the lights from inside glowing parts of his face. I cough. "Let me take you out for a coffee to thank you?"

He tilts his head slightly to the side, the only change in emotion he offers me. "I don't let girls take me out. I take them out."

I control the excitement begging to burst further through my body, and channel my inner confidence as much as I can. "Then take me out," I offer a small smile.

The corner of his mouth lifts slightly, and he moves closer to me, filling the space between us. We now share each other's warm breath, fighting away the cold air around us. My heart beats fiercely inside my chest with anticipation. There must be something truly wrong with me to be feeling this way. I was nearly raped and then watched him stab a man in front of my eyes. I should be an inconsolable mess on the ground, but here I am; feeling emotions I have not felt in such a long time.

"Something tells me I couldn't afford to take you out Petal, now leave this town before something worse happens to you." He smirks down at me, his build towering over me and making me feel much smaller than I did with the other three guys.

"Won't you be there to save me again?"

His eyes flicker back to that emotionless calm. "I'm not the saving type," he walks away and leaves me alone once more.

I'm not the saving type.

Why did those words spark something further inside me?

Chapter Five

Isobel

Lewis is parked around the corner, listening to a podcast. He never left the parking lot, and the thought of him finding out what could have happened while he sat not far away would have destroyed him. I decide not to tell him anything at all. I use the portable mirror in my bag to straighten out my hair and rub the smudges of dirt from my face. He pauses his podcast as I hop into the back of the car, the warmth from the heaters encasing every inch of my body; I hum at the comfort. "Back to The Lodge?"

"Yes, please Lewis."

"We still leaving tomorrow, Miss?"

"Lewis, please just call me Isobel, and yes we are." I rest my head back against the comfortable leather seat.

He smiles in the mirror. "I will try."

"What were you listening to?"

He pulls out of the parking lot, driving towards the main road, where soon the cozy wood heater would carry me to a warmful sleep. He seems to be blushing slightly, "they are called *Let Them Fight*."

"I have never heard of them before."

"They talk about different people that have had a violent history and they make dark humorous jokes the entire time."

I smile, "I didn't take you for a dark humour kind of guy Lewis."

"We all have our secrets," his tone is smiling now and less embarrassed.

That we do Lewis. That we do. I don't answer him, and we remain silent for the rest of the drive, only for him to tell me goodnight and that he will be waiting down here ready for me.

Getting back to my empty room is a different feeling entirely. In the wall to floor mirror, I watch myself as I remove my coat, only to see the evidence of their attempted attack. My shirt is ripped in so many areas, revealing my bra and stomach, and as I discard it altogether; I see the bruises already forming on my skin. Especially on my arms, I am sure my legs have plenty too. I suck in a shaky breath as I strip completely naked, taking in the damage.

I can see the bruise indents from their fingertips, going a deep shade of purple, bruising on my legs and ass as well, along with my collarbone. I must have fought harder that I thought. I graze my hands over the bruising, my mind flashing with each rip and touch from their unwanted hands, hands that I now picture chopping off. I open my eyes to see the tears spilling over as my breathing becomes more erratic. I touch the back of my head, wincing at the soreness before bringing my fingertips to my eyes. There is a small amount of blood from knocking my head against the ground.

I walk to the bathroom, turning the shower on and waiting for it to heat before I slide to the floor, letting the water attempt to wash their stains away. The bruises on my skin will be a constant reminder for a while, but I try to remember the reminders they will have. Broken bones and stab wounds. It didn't feel like enough now that I am alone.

If she was my girl, you would already be dead.

My shaking body calms as I relish in the feeling of them being hurt, as I replay their screams in my mind as Atlas tore into them with ease. Then I close my eyes and picture him doing more. I picture him breaking every bone in their body, then tying their broken bodies to trees, and letting the wolves finish them. I picture their unanswered screams as they are slowly eaten alive.

I sigh in relief, yes that feels like a fitting end for their crime.

After crying some more while watching American Horror Story, I eventually fall to sleep.

Hands paw at my clothes, ripping away my dignity with ease. This time I don't stop screaming, I scream so loud that my voice cracks. "Please!" I beg over and over. "Please," I cry. I don't want this to happen. "Please," I moan. I look down to green eyes between my legs.

"What was that, Petal?"

"Please don't stop," I beg.

He smirks before dropping his head back between my legs.

I wake with a jolt. My breathing hitched and tiny tingles have made their way across my body. Did I have an orgasm in my sleep? The room is still dark and I try to push away the fact that I had a dream that started with rape and ended with his eyes and a wet dream.

What the actual fuck is wrong with me?

But I had an orgasm, I'm sure of it. I reach for my water bottle and my phone, it is only 4am. I take a large gulp of water. It has been so very long since I had felt it, so long that part of me is almost tempted to touch myself, to see if I can bring on another one.

I decide instead to check social media, replying to a few fans every now and then, but my mind is constantly plagued by his light green eyes. I am attracted to him, something I haven't had for so long, but it is more than just an attraction. I feel something with him, a nervous kind of electricity, like the currents are unstable. Like I know that there is a chance I will be shocked and my heart will stop, but at least it is feeling something. Suddenly, those three girls that stole from me don't seem scary, or those three guys that pinned me down and threatened to take the last bit of me with them, no that doesn't terrify me. The true fear is the thought of returning home and not feeling that spark. It scares me imagining my heart remaining without excitement.

But I felt it brewing at the bottom of my stomach with him.

Felt the intensity of his gaze on mine, of the way the anticipation clawed at my heart when he shared my breath. Wanting, actually wanting for him to kiss me even after the attack, I wanted a man's hands on me. And if I go home tomorrow, there is a good chance I will never see him again, a good chance that I won't feel those emotions ever again, that my heart will remain lost, only beating for survival and not for the true purpose of living.

I open the curtains and watch the orange sunrise light up the green trees around me, knowing that there is no way I can go home without seeing him once more.

I need to feel that electricity, that reason for living, I need him before all of me is gone forever.

CHAPTER SIX

ISOBEL

I hope with everything that he is at the bar again tonight, if he isn't, I have no way of finding him, and how long do I spend in this town waiting for him to show up? I spent the day writing, and surprisingly, I got a solid thousand words done. Lately I can only get around a hundred after hours of staring blankly at my screen, hoping for inspiration to come, but it doesn't. Really, I don't need to write ever again if I didn't want to, but I love it. Writing is a part of my soul, another part of me that has disappeared that I have been desperate to hold on to.

Changing into jeans, a knit and a thick scarf, I am confronted again by the bruises. Bruises that are taking on a darker shade of purple, with a light blue spreading my skin. My eyes sting with the memories that plague my mind, but I push them away. I would not shed more tears for those kinds of men. The kind that didn't even deserve the title man, they are nothing more than cowardly monsters.

Lewis seemed a little shocked when I rang him in the morning that we would be staying, but he says nothing as I get into the car tonight, the weather becoming so cool; I feel it will begin snowing as the end of autumn approaches.

Walking into the same bar for the third night in a row, I look only for him, and although my panic picks up as I take in the now familiar area of what led to the bruises on my body; a reassuring calm feels me as I see him in his usual seat. Before the nerves drive me back to Chicago, I begin walking to him without thinking, without giving myself the chance to change my mind. Because a strong part of me knows, knows without a doubt that Atlas is not a good man, but a stronger part of me doesn't care. The part of me that wants to feel that excitement, that in a year only he has made me feel. One whole year of waiting for something more, something to bring the desire back to my body, back to my soul. I would not walk away from that, damn the cost; my heart can take a bad man if it means feeling alive.

"Try me."

He turns to face me, his eyebrows raising with confusion.

"See if you can take me out," I offer a small smile.

"Persistent aren't you, Petal."

"My name is Isobel," I say as I feel the warmth creep up my neck, warmth that I thought was gone forever.

He wears a plain white shirt with denim jeans, but begins reaching for his coat hanging behind his bar stool. "You won't complain about having a beer over some fancy Cristal?"

I fight the irritation that he thinks he knows me already. "Try me," I repeat with a fake sweet smile.

His smirk grows. "Okay Petal," he extends his hand for me to lead the way out of here. I hope to never come back, and a scary part of me thought maybe he would just take us to the dining area to test me, to see if I really wouldn't complain.

I told Lewis to go back to The Lodge so that I could avoid him seeing me leave with Atlas. I wasn't sure if I was ready for judgment and questions. He leads me to a faded blue pickup truck, opening the passenger door and waiting for me to get in before he closes it. The few seconds of silence before he gets in the driver's side are filled with my pulse beating loudly in my ears. What was I doing?

But did it even matter? I was feeling excitement just from being in his truck. Too late to turn back now. I wonder as he starts the engine if he felt any of the things that I have, or if he is merely following through because I have made myself so easy. I guess that is the risk I took getting in a car with a complete stranger.

We stay in silence as he drives us through the night, away from the area of town that I am staying, and further through this side of town. "Regrets Petal?"

"It's Isobel, and no, no complaints here," I offer him that sweet smile again.

"Keep giving me that fake smile, and I will have you begging for longer," his jaw moves with his lazy smirk.

"Begging for what?" I whisper, but he doesn't answer me, and I'm taken back to my dream; the dream of his head between my thighs. I clench them together, but he notices and he chuckles at the way my body responds to him.

Old me would have walked away from his arrogant ego within seconds, the old me would have let him chase. But the new me, the one that had been broken, was just excited to be feeling this reaction. A scary thought crosses my mind as we sink back into silence. I was about to let this man do whatever he wanted with me, just so that I could continue feeling the flutters grow.

We pull into a trailer park and I suck in a breath at what I thought my expectations would be. "You are taking me to your home?" I ask nervously.

"You wanted somewhere more public?"

It's like this man has forgotten I was nearly raped last night, has forgotten how easily he rescued me, bringing harm to those three men in a way I have never seen someone do before. "Your home is fine," I reply quietly, enjoying the flutters assaulting my stomach. Just us, completely alone.

He rushes to grab my door for me, and I wait patiently, not wanting to rob him of this chivalrous act. He leads me up the four small stairs leading to his trailer, which looks far more put together than the other ones in the area. He opens the door and I am immediately taken aback by what I see. It is like he has hand built everything in here, mostly everything is a dark wood, he has installed a tiny black wood heater that has a pot for coffee on top; he has fairy lights hanging around the small area of his home, but my eyes are drawn to where the small two-seater table is set with a fake flickering candle, a vase of purple carnations, two wine glasses poured, and two bowls wrapped with aluminium foil. My mouth opens with surprise. "You knew...I would come back?" I don't even bother to hide the shock from my voice.

"Yes," he says simply, shutting the door behind us.

I unwrap my scarf as I walk closer to the table, "how?" It seems like the only reasonable question.

"I saw the way you looked at me," he smiles.

I roll my eyes, "cocky much?"

He raises his eyebrows to me as if to say, we both know I am good looking. Which isn't a lie, just like I know that I am beautiful. It's not something I would ever pretend to deny or act like I am unsure of. He gestures for me to take a seat, and I do, unwrapping the foil on my bowl, revealing a thick stew. The smell of rosemary and garlic invades my senses as he unwraps the garlic bread in between us. "You made all this?"

He nods, and I dip my spoon in, attempting to grab every vegetable and the meat in one bite. The tender meat collapses in my mouth and my eyes close as I let out a small hum. I reach for a garlic bread, and realise that this is honestly one of the nicest things that has ever been done for me by a guy. "Thank you, for all this." Maybe my radar was off when I thought he was a bad guy, but still he hurt those others with ease, and he also told me to fuck off the first time we met. Confusion creeps inside my mind as I attempt to figure Atlas out.

"So why is a rich girl like you coming to the same shitty bar every night?"

"Well, if you actually let me speak on our first encounter, you would have known."

I see him resisting the urge to smile. "You have an attitude; you know that right?"

"Is that a problem?" I challenge.

"Oh no, I will very much enjoy taking the time to fix it," he places a bite full in his mouth, and my cheeks heat at his words.

I sip at my wine in an attempt to hide my embarrassment. "I am looking for my father actually," I reach for my phone to show him the picture. His face remains the same as he looks.

"Never seen him before."

"He has been missing for a few months now. The police have pretty well given up on ever finding him," I sigh.

"Do you know why he was here?"

"No, none whatsoever."

"Is he the reason you have money?"

I give him that fake smile again, the one I know that irritates him. He returns my smile with his own knowing smirk. "Have you heard of *Them or Us*?"

"Like the movie series?" he reaches for his wine.

I nod my head, "yes well before it was a movie, it was a book, written by me;" I cannot help but smile smugly. Screw his expectations of me.

He whistles. "You made your own money."

"Is that such a shock?"

"Not at all, I just enjoy getting under your skin, Petal."

I ignore the constant use of this nickname he has given me. "What is it you do?" Changing the subject away from myself.

"I work at the Mill just outside of town, cutting down wood."
I guess that explained the muscles. My eyes flicker to his arms, and
I can't help but picture how easy it would be for him to pick me
up.

"Are you close to your dad?"

The personal question catches me off-guard. "Not for a long
time, not since I was little, actually."

"So why go to all this effort for him?"

I had been asking myself the same question, especially after last
night. "I hate not knowing, I hate waiting for answers that no one
seems willing to find. I needed to do something, anything, to stop
my racing thoughts of all the what ifs."

"Will you keep looking or go home?"

"I will leave soon." I don't tell him that I was meant to leave
today, but the thought of seeing him again stopped me.

"And where is home?"

"Chicago," my spoon scrapes along the bottom of my bowl,
lapping up the last of the delicious dinner.

"So our time is limited?"

"Is that a problem?" I return one of his smirks and his own
grows.

CHAPTER SEVEN

ISOBEL

He reaches under my chair, and with ease slides it close to his own, his mouth so close to mine that our lips are almost touching. "What is it you want from me, Petal?" He whispers against my lips.

A throb seems to travel from my chest and settle between my legs. How does he make me feel this way without even doing anything?

"I'm not sure," I answer honestly, my eyes moving from his, then down to his lips.

"You don't seem like the kind of girl that would seek my attention," he moves his mouth to my neck, lightly brushing his lips against me, and I can't help the small noise that leaves my throat.

"You keep making expectations about who you think I am," I reply firmly, trying not to break my gaze from his.

"I am going to tell you right now that I'm not the kind of man you settle down with, I'm cruel and dangerous...but you already know that, don't you Petal?"

"Yes," I breathe, intoxicated by the way his eyes hold mine.

He runs his finger down my cheek, "and do I scare you?"

"Yes," I answer honestly.

"But you enjoy that, don't you?" His other hand slowly moves up my thigh. "It turns you on, the uncertainty?"

I nod my head, all words getting lodged in my throat. "Always answer me Petal," his voice has turned firm.

"Yes," I answer again.

He smiles at my compliance, before moving my knit down to reveal some of the bruising. "Do you want to know the real reason I knew you would come back demanding this date?"

"More than just your good looks?" I grin.

"You stayed and watched, and at first, I thought maybe it was just the shock that kept you from running, but I soon realised that you needed to watch me punish them, you enjoyed their pain. Most people would in your circumstance, but when I came over to you, I realised in that moment that you wanted to be afraid of me, you would have let me fuck you right then after all those pieces of shit tried to do to you; it didn't break you."

I remain silent and unbreathing, at a loss for how observant he is, and how truly fucked up I sound. "It made me so curious as to what would break you, this girl that is turned on by violence, this girl that looked at her attackers with dead eyes, this girl that would let me fuck her in the cold of the night just after being hurt. So, no Petal, I have no expectations of you, in fact; I am completely in awe of you."

"Because I was excited at the fact that I watched you stab someone for me?"

"Because you are not just a bored little rich girl looking for some excitement. No, you might quite possibly be just as fucked up as me. It took all my strength not to kiss you last night."

"Why didn't you?"

"Because look at my life, he gestures to the trailer he lives in. You aren't someone I can be obsessed with."

"Obsessed?" This man is a walking red flag, but I already knew that before I came here.

"I can be quite possessive with what I deem mine, and you have a very different life from me. I debated not even going back to the bar, thinking you would surely leave this town if I wasn't, but I couldn't remove your dark, dead eyes from my mind."

Ironic that I felt the same about his. "I'm glad you came back," I whisper.

He leans in, lightly brushing his lips against my own as my breath catches. With the way he consumes my air, I know that from this kiss onward, I will always be trying to catch my breath around him. He presses harder, spreading my mouth open for his tongue to push in, his hand moving to the back of my neck. A part of me was nervous about kissing someone for the first time in a year, like I might be sloppy at it, but with Atlas; it is no less than perfect.

If this is how our lips mould together, I can't even imagine the rest of our bodies.

I can't help the little moan that leaves my mouth, and he grins against my lips; knowing exactly what he is doing to me, taking his time to draw out both of our pleasure. I bite down on his bottom lip impatiently, and he sits back, his tongue darting out to taste the small drop of blood I left. His eyes dance before me, his smirk growing to something truly dangerous. "Oh, you should not have done that Petal." Quicker than I have time to react, he is lifting me and carrying me the four steps to his bed. It feels effortless to be in his arms as I wrap my legs around his waist, fisting his hair as our lips collide again; this time there is nothing gentle about the way our mouths meet. I need all of him, and from the feel of his dick pressed against his jeans, I know he feels the same.

I am about to let this stranger do whatever he wants to me, as long as it keeps my heart bashing against my chest, as long as I can feel that desire trying to claw its way out of me. I need this release, need it to be him that causes it. "Atlas," I breathe, needing him to know I am ready for more. Removing my shirt and bra with ease, he lays me on his bed, his eyes darkening as he begins unbuttoning my jeans and tugging them down. I lift my hips to help him remove my panties. I wore a silky Victoria's Secret set, and suddenly I realise that I am completely naked while he remains clothed. "This isn't fair," I whisper, reaching for his shirt, but he shoves me back down.

"Fucking beautiful," his eyes roam my body greedily, and I begin to squirm. "So impatient, Petal," he grins. Sliding a hand into his back pocket, he pulls out a pocket knife, rotating it between his fingers with the ease of someone who has spent hours practicing.

"Atlas," I warn shakily, fear flicking to the knife he glides between each finger.

Then he spreads one of my legs with his knee and settles onto me, the tip of the knife touching my cheek. "I can feel your terrified heart beating, are you scared Petal?"

"Yes," I swallow at my dry throat, my eyes never leaving his.

Slowly, he begins trailing the knife down my neck, gliding to my breasts, the tip nothing more than a tickle on my skin, but a promise of what he could do to me lies heavy in my thumping chest. Then he places my nipple in his mouth and I arch into his touch with a hiss, his tongue swirling and teeth lightly grazing as I move my hands back into his hair. I had forgotten what this feels like, but my body is so alive, like it is on the greatest high of life. He moves his fingers between my legs, before stopping and quickly moving away from me. I whimper at the loss of contact.

"You aren't wet," he says, concerned.

Heat rises to my cheeks in embarrassment, and I close my legs. I forgot to tell him; well, it isn't something you exactly tell a stranger. "I- um, my body doesn't get wet."

"What do you mean?" He has moved a metre away from me, standing a bit back from the bed.

"It's called vaginismus," my eyes move away from his with shame.

"I have never heard of it."

"It just means I can't get wet and that my body is always tensing down there," I cough, drawing my knees up to my chest. "I'm sorry if you find it unappealing," I take in how far from me he has moved and how quickly. Like he is repulsed by me now.

"I thought you weren't into it, into me." It is hard to imagine Atlas as the kind of man that is ever worried. "Do you want this?" He steps a little closer again, and I reach out for him.

"This is the first time I have wanted this in a very long time, in fact, I think it is the most I have ever wanted something."

He grins, ripping my legs to the end of the bed and spreading them while he stands between me. "I like to leave marks, these bruises covering your body should be from me. Is that something you think you can handle, Petal?"

I nod nervously, that fluttering returning between my legs. "We might just need some lube-"

He throws the knife into the air, purposely catching the blade side, I gasp with worry. "Atlas," I begin to reach for him but he shoves me down aggressively. Then I watch as he holds his hand between my legs and his blood drips onto my clit, sliding down.

The warmth tickles me as my eyes open wide with shock. "What-"

But my words are choked down as he moves the handle of the blade between my thighs. "Uhh-I'm not sure about this..." I can hardly think as I feel the tip of the knife handle against me. He moves the blood around my entrance, and I grip the sheets with anticipation.

"Do you know what knife this is?" He still moves it around, the blood lubricating the area, and I begin to squirm, wanting him to push into me. Actually, wanting the knife inside me.

Jesus Christ.

"The one you used to save me?"

He smiles and pushes into me; I gasp out in pleasure and shock. He holds the blade, making sure that the edges don't touch me. I look down as he begins fucking me with the knife, his own blood trickling further down his arm and onto the sheets as he grips the blade to fuck me harder. "How does it feel to have the knife I used to punish those mean inside you?"

I moan, clutching the sheets tighter. "It feels powerful," I admit.

"I knew you would enjoy it Petal, I see you better than you see yourself."

"Atlas," I moan.

"Look how nicely your pussy swallows my knife." I look down to see more of his blood on my thighs, the sight bringing me close to the edge.

"Even though I will enjoy marking you Petal, I will bleed for you whenever you need me to."

"Oh god I'm close," I hold my breath as the pressure builds.

"Cum for me like the good girl you are," I explode beneath him, my first real orgasm dragging out longer than I have ever felt.

He removes the knife, and my eyes grow heavy. "Your hand," I begin to reach for it, but he places it against my cheek; his thumb lightly stroking.

"You did so good," I smile at his gentle words and touch, my head feeling heavy from sitting up. He moves me up against the pillow and tucks the blanket over my naked body.

"It will be impossible not to be obsessed with you," he whispers, the feeling of his hand stroking my head as I fall deep into sleep.

CHAPTER EIGHT

ISOBEL

I wake to dark wood and dark sheets, feeling a little disoriented as I sit up, still completely naked. "Atlas?" I call out to no answer. Beside me on the table is a note,

-Petal, I will be back soon.

I stretch out my arms as I hear my phone vibrating. "Oh no," I jump out of the bed, flinging myself towards my bag. 52 missed calls from Lewis. "Shit, shit, shit!" My shaking hands begin dialling him back.

"Miss Isobel!?" His voice is full of panic.

"Lewis! I am so sorry!"

"Are you okay?" His tone is shaky.

"I am completely fine; I am turning on my location for you to come pick me up." I hang up and rush to find my discarded clothes, before dashing into the bathroom, the only room that is separate from everything else in the trailer. My hair is a mess and my cheek is caked with dry blood. I scrub at my face, and tie my hair in a messy bun in an attempt to hide the evidence of what I let happen last night.

I wait outside, Lewis comes flying into the park, skidding the tyres as he hits the dirt. Thank God I messaged Bre that I wouldn't be home, or I would have had the police looking for me. I hop into the car before he has time to get out. "What the fuck!"

It is the first time I have heard Lewis swear. "Lewis, I am truly so sorry," I shut the door, and he has turned to face me, his eyes holding a fierce anger. Which is completely understandable.

"I thought you were dead!"

"I-" My cheeks warm as I remember my night, how I completely passed out from having the most incredible orgasm of my life, not something I can tell my driver.

"Just message me, if you are going to be spending the night somewhere," his cheeks have turned bright red, as we both sit together after my walk of shame.

"I can't even imagine what I have put you through, truly I am so sorry," I say sincerely, because if someone did that to me; I would be livid.

"When will we be going home?" He has turned his attention back to the front, as he drives the car out of the trailer park. My eyes dart back to Atlas's house, what would he think when he gets back, and I am gone?

"I will look at flights tomorrow," and just as I lean my head back against the leather seat, snow begins to fall outside; flittering down as it gently hits the windshield.

Back inside the warmth of The Lodge, I flick on the news as the weather outside becomes angry. The wind fiercely pushing against every surface, desperately trying to find a way in; as the snow and ice rip into the windows. Although the flames from the wood heater dart higher from the wind moving down the flue, a chill spreads across my body.

"A blizzard is set to move across these states." I drown out the reporter as my head moves to look out the window, watching trees take on the coming assault of nature's most feared elements; minus fire.

I sigh, is this some sort of fucked up sign? I had tried not to let my mind wander to Atlas, to the way his blood coated my thighs and how it made me feel. I had never experienced anything like it before, as I am sure most human beings haven't. It wasn't exactly a normal sexual interaction to have, but I enjoyed it...admitting that scares me more than the knife he placed inside me. Scares me, because what if I am now fucked up beyond repair? I enjoyed the way that even though he had all the control; he was the one hurting, not me. Does that make me sick? The eerie feeling of wanting more had caused me to look at flights as soon as we got home, but now with this blizzard. I sigh again.

Bre's name lights up on my phone, and I reach to answer it.

"You should have come home yesterday," she says.

"I know," I admit, keeping my eyes on the unforgiving weather.

"You will have to tell your mum."

"I'm working myself up to it."

"What made you stay the extra day?"

I walk back to the bed, sitting on the edge, wondering how much I should tell Bre. Knowing that in itself is another huge red flag. "There is this guy..."

"TELL. ME. EVERYTHING."

"It's new, but I- I feel something with him."

Bre lets out an excited breath, knowing how big of a deal this is. She is the only one that knows what happened to me. "Have you guys?"

"Not yet, but I want to Bre, for the first time in a year."

"I want to meet him!"

"It is a little early for that," I smile.

"Would he move back to Chicago with you?"

"Bre! We have had one date, no one is moving anywhere. I- I don't know if he is right for me..."

"What's that supposed to mean?" Her tone has changed to worry.

"I think he is a little fucked up." I want to say a lot fucked up, but that would come with more questions.

She goes silent for a moment. "Iz, you are a little fucked up," she says gently.

"I know," I whisper.

"Maybe...you need someone fucked up, someone that can understand?"

"Maybe," I admit.

"Just don't put any pressure on yourself, and trust the way you feel, okay?"

"Okay, I miss you Bre."

"I miss you too Iz, let me know how your mum takes the news, and keep me updated on everything."

"I will," I promise.

"And Iz?"

"Yes?"

"Trust the fanny flutters."

I choke out a laugh. "You said that we needed to trust our head now that we are older."

"Mm, yeah, well, for you, things are a little different. If your body is finally telling you something; I think you should trust it."

I definitely think I shouldn't. "Love you."

"Love you too, see you soon," and then she hangs up.

I decide to spend the rest of the day writing; the words typing out with a strange ease, an ease that has been lost for so long; I was almost ready to give up. A part of my brain knows it must be because of Atlas, and that is enough to cause me to chew at the skin on my fingers.

I message Lewis to meet me down at the restaurant for dinner, feeling guilty about last night and also knowing he is probably getting a little lonely here. I pay him extremely well to be my driver, and I picked him because of the comfortable feeling the features on his face brought me. He is twenty-three, a year older than me, and he has this adorably shy demeanour about him. "Miss Isobel," he says, smiling as he greets me.

"Lewis, please for the love of God, just call me Isobel, or Iz, I think after everything I put you through last night; that you are entitled to it."

"I will try," his anger has all faded away, as his shyness spreads across his face.

There are plenty of seats vacant, so we sit beside a window, watching the weather violently thrash around. I can't help but think that a blizzard has got to be the biggest sign that has ever been thrown at me. It is literally stopping me from leaving this town, from leaving Atlas, who will probably never talk to me again after running out of his house while he was gone. Lewis orders a steak and I order a pasta, both of us opting for a red wine with our meals. "Do you have anyone special back home?" We knew things about each other, but not an excessive amount of personal details. He knows why I am in this town, but we don't go out of our ways to pry into each other's lives.

"No Mi- Isobel," he smiles before cutting into more of his steak.

"Has there ever been? Don't feel like you need to tell me if you don't want," I smile reassuringly.

"Yeah, there was," he smiles sadly. "It got toxic, and I ended up leaving the state."

"What kind of toxic?"

"The kind where she burnt all my shit and took a baseball bat to my car."

"Jesus Lewis," my mouth pops open.

He shrugs, "I may have slept with her brother by accident."

My jaw may as well be touching the table. Innocent Lewis is not so innocent after all. "How do you accidentally sleep with someone?"

"Well, I didn't really know at that time that I found guys attractive. She wanted us to bond and obviously we took that a little too far. The guilt was too heavy, and I ended up confessing to her the truth."

"So you're bi?"

He places another chunk of steak into his mouth, shrugging again. "I don't really bother with labels. I fuck men and women," he says simply.

I hide my choke on a sip of wine. "So, there was no one after the uh brother and sister?"

"No, I think I loved him. I thought I loved her but it didn't compare to what I felt with him, I'm sure he has moved on now."

"I could write a book about you, Lewis."

His eyes flash with humour. "Do I get any of the royalties?" He teases.

"Hmm, no, but I could put you in my acknowledgements."

"Who was the mystery trailer park, man or woman?"

I realise that Lewis has never seen me with either, only Bre or my mother. "He is kind of intense," I admit.

"That is the best kind," he sips his wine.

"You think so?"

"Of course, all the passion comes from intensity. So, he is the reason we are still in this town?"

"He was the reason we stayed the extra night; I found out nothing about my father."

He offers me a sad smile. "I'm sorry Isobel," my eyes light up with him using my name without the fancy title in front. "That felt wrong," he smiles and I laugh loudly.

"You know Lewis, sometimes I think I need another friend more than a driver. It is hard when people realise you are rich, to find who is truly there for you and who wants the money."

He pauses for a moment, "I can be both Isobel."

We go back to our rooms after one more wine, and I found myself laughing more than usual, something only Bre can bring out of me; and even she has struggled this past year. I place the hotel card on the hall table before heading to the bathroom, feeling the desire to soak into the spa bath. I stop my walking, as something catches my eyes. I retrace my steps a couple paces and look at my bedside table. Sitting in a small vase is a bunch of purple carnations.

CHAPTER NINE

ISOBEL

I gasp, feeling the warmth of him behind me, I quickly turn to find him looking down at me with a smile. "How did you get in here?" I breathe.

"Your bags are packed," he says instead.

I attempt to create some space between us, but he follows my sidestep, leaving me with nowhere but a wall behind me. "Yes, well, I needed to pack my bags in order to leave."

"You would leave without saying goodbye, Petal?" He backs me against the wall and my heart rate picks up.

"You didn't answer my question," I hold my ground.

"You will find that it is extremely hard to escape me."

I swallow down my fear. "I was going to go, but the blizzard stopped me."

"I asked for you to be delayed," he grins. Like he is suggesting that he is the one that caused this blizzard.

I scoff, "you aren't a God."

"And when you cried out for him with my knife inside you, whose face were you looking at?"

"I-" He smirks at my loss of words. I roll my eyes as he moves his hand to my throat, lightly grazing his thumb against my windpipe.

"And who is it you worship, Petal?" His thumb on my windpipe begins pushing down.

"No one," I say defiantly.

He cocks his head to the side, his hand wrapping tightly against my throat, stopping the air from getting to my lungs. I watch him with unwavering eyes, and he holds my own, his hand getting tighter as I begin to feel panic.

My eyes growing wide only further his smile, his grip not loosening as I begin to feel lightheaded, small black dots begin clouding my vision. He lets go and I greedily suck in all the air I was denied, before his thumb is lightly stroking my throat once more. "Who do you worship?"

"You," I whisper.

"Prove it," he smiles darkly.

My legs feel wobbly as I drop to my knees before him, reaching for the button on his jeans with shaky hands. He helps me free his dick, and I suck in a breath at the size of him. "Oh god," I breathe. There is no way I will be able to take all of him in my mouth.

"I rather like this name you have given me," he smirks.

"I- I haven't done this for a long time," I whisper.

"You have three seconds to decide whether you will be choking from my dick or my hands, Petal."

I lick my lips again before placing him in my mouth, letting him fill me as far as I can take him before I start moving my head. He groans, grabbing the back of my neck; a fistful of my hair weaving between his fingers.

He moans loudly as I flick my tongue along the sensitive tip, before dipping my head back along the length of him, choking as I try to take him further. "Eyes on me, Petal," I lift my eyes to his, my thighs pressing against each other as I take in the desperate desire he holds while watching me. His soft moans giving me all the encouragement I need to pick up my pace. "Fuck baby, you suck me so good," I moan around him at the use of the word baby. Delighting in how I am making him feel. "I'm going to cum down your throat, and you are going to swallow every last drop." I move my head faster, watching as his eyes close and his grip on my neck tightens, knowing he is nearly finished. "Fuck," he groans and the warmth from him squirts to the back of my throat. His eyes opening to watch me swallow of all him, his breath is heavy as he thrusts a couple more times into my mouth before removing himself.

His hand moves from the back of my neck to the side of my eye, swiping away the tear; and then resting his thumb against my cheek. "You did so good," he whispers to me. Reaching down, he lifts me into his arms and cradles me against his chest, on the edge of the bed.

"How did I taste Petal?" He moves his thumb against my lips, swiping along the bottom.

Instead of answering him, I press my lips against his, opening my mouth and sliding my tongue along his, letting him taste his salty cum.

He groans his approval. "I want my cum in and on every part of your body. I want every man to know that you are marked as mine."

"I'm yours?" I ask, feeling the tears build. I wasn't sure why I feel like crying over that. Maybe because the thought of someone wanting me as theirs after all that happened seems impossible.

He doesn't know what happened.

Maybe he wouldn't want me if he did. "Do you know what that means?" He kisses the tear building at the side of my eye.

"No one else can have me?"

"If you let another man touch you, I will kill them Petal, is that understood?"

A memory of him easily attacking those three men flashes before my eyes. He means it, he truly means what he is saying, and maybe I should feel repulsed. Maybe I should run so far he will never find me, but the growing familiarity of my heart thumping with him around is back, and I never want it to stop; I never want to lose this new part of me. The part that can write again, the part that laughed with Lewis at dinner. The part that feels alive for the first time in a year.

"You might not want me if you knew everything about me," I whisper. He sits me on the bed and disappears into the bathroom before I hear him turning on the taps for the spa bath.

"I could say the same about me, Isobel," and my heart swells at the use of my name for the first time. He reaches for my knit, tugging the cream cashmere above my head. He places a light kiss against my neck as he unclasps my bra with one hand. Freeing my breasts, he places a kiss against both. "I am so going to enjoy getting to know every part of you."

He pushes my back against the bed. "Does this mean you will kneel for me also?" I find his eyebrows pulling together, like he is fighting something within himself.

"I will worship you in every way Petal, but I will never kneel for anyone," he says firmly. I push down the hurt for now, and watch as he tugs off my pants and slides down my panties. "Fucking perfect," he whispers.

I stand before him, reaching for his shirt, and he doesn't stop me this time. I slide it up over his head, but he needs to help me lift it all the way with his towering height. I take in his tan skin, covered with different patch work tattoos, but my breath catches with all the scars that line his body. With shaky hands, I trace my fingers along his firm muscles, before lightly kissing his chest like he did to me. "Perfect," my lips whisper against his skin and I risk glancing up at him, at the face that watches me like no one else has before. At the desire and pain mixed through his green eyes. I slide his jeans and underwear back down, he steps out of them before picking me up and carrying me to the bath, sliding us both in with my back nestled against his chest, I hum as the hot water caresses me.

He turns the jets on, the noise loudly bubbles around us, as I sink further back against his chest. "What are you thinking about?" he begins tracing his watery fingers along my collarbone.

I close my eyes as the bubbling water massages my body. "I guess about how strange all this is."

"You think I'm strange?"

I open my eyes and tilt my head to look at his face, he is smiling. "You think you're normal?" I challenge.

"Being normal is a luxury," he says, and I rest my head back against his chest.

"I know nothing about you, but I feel like there is no one else I would have let do that to me," I blush as I remember his blood on my thighs. I look down at his hand and notice the Steri-Strips he has closing the wound.

"What happened to you, Isobel?"

"Hmm?"

"I researched Vaginismus, causes are trauma involved with sex or with childbirth. Do you have a kid I don't know about?"

"No," I whisper, the jets drowning my voice out.

"Then what happened?"

"I-it's not something I want to talk about."

He tilts my chin up to look at him. "I want to know every single thing about you Petal, nothing you will say can ever scare me off; understand?"

I nod my head and turn back away from him. "It was just over a year ago now, I um- I was with my father and his brother, who has a son. My cousin is a year older than me, and because I never saw my dad that often, I never had much of a relationship with my uncle or cousin either; not since I was a kid, anyway." I suck in a shaky breath, and his fingers continue to trail my skin in a soothing way. "We all got extremely drunk together, the drunkest I have ever been, my father placed me in the spare room when I passed out. I can vaguely remember him tucking me in." I begin to panic, my breathing becoming more erratic as I attempt to get through the rest of the story.

"Hey," He whispers, turning my head with his finger under my chin. My breaths are still leaving my lungs too quickly, and he claims them with his mouth. Kissing away my terror, owning my fear with his own breath, absorbing it into his body. "I'm here, Petal," he whispers against my mouth.

I nod my head, swallowing down the tremors as I brush away a tear, wetting my face more with the process. "I woke up to my cousin's dick in my mouth," I say with disgust. His trailing only stops for a second. "When I started to come to, I was so drunk I couldn't move, hardly an inch as I began to scream. He put his hand over my mouth and told me that both our fathers had gone out for more drinks, that we were all alone." I fight off the pain in my throat as it begins to restrict. "He then started fingering me, I sloppily begged him to stop in my drunken state. I can still remember the feeling of begging my body to move, to fight him off; but I was hardly able to stay conscious. And then he fucked me while I cried, begging myself to fall unconscious again at that point. When I came to, my underwear and pants gone and his- I walked to a pharmacy and purchased the morning-after pill."

I sniff and rub my nose as he remains silent behind me, but I can feel his body heating, feel the simmering of his soul into mine. "Did you tell your father?" His voice is cold.

"No, I- I just left. I never saw him again. I think he may have known something happened because I refused to see him in fear of my cousin and uncle being there."

"Is that why you are here? Because you feel guilty that you didn't see him again and now he has gone missing?"

"I think yes, a part of me does wish I saw him again, but I also know that he wasn't a good father. He was never there enough and even when he was there, I wasn't protected," my bottom lip wobbles but I control my sadness. "Part of me just wants to know, so that I can put all of this to rest and move on with my life."

"Did you ever tell anyone about your cousin?"

"Only my friend Bre."

"So, he got away with hurting you?" His anger simmers in the bubbling water once more as I nod my head.

"I was so disgusted and ashamed that I couldn't bring myself to tell my mum."

"You have nothing to be ashamed of Isobel, you are a warrior," he says proudly.

"You don't- want me less?" The fear moves into my blood at the thought of him being disgusted by me.

"Petal, I will want you more every day, every day you give me; my desire will only grow." I feel his dick grow hard beneath me, proving his words true.

"Tell me something about you now," needing to distract myself from the burning feeling spreading through my core.

"I was a Navy Seal." His fingers dip from my collarbone, beginning to trace my nipple.

My breath hitches. "Navy Seal," I say, almost in disbelief. "That makes sense," I arch back further into his touch.

"Does it now Petal?"

"Y-yes, the way you fought those guys. It was so easy for you," his hand begins trailing lower.

"When I tell you that if any other man touches you like this, that I will kill them; I mean it. I know of a great many ways to kill, of how to do it quickly." His fingers begin gently rubbing my clit. "And how to take my time," he whispers against my ear and I moan, pushing further back against his chest. "How to cause the most amount of pain before they meet their end," he slips one finger inside me and I clutch at his thigh.

"Atlas," I breathe.

"I can feel it," he whispers, his finger curling up with ease in this position.

"What?" I moan louder, my nails digging into his skin.

"Your perfect cunt tightening around my finger- you are so fucking tight Petal," he slips in a second finger. "I am going to have so much fun stretching you, we have something much bigger to fit than my fingers." His dick twitches behind me and I gasp, gripping his thigh tighter.

"Tell me Petal, have you been with anyone in this past year?"

"No," I moan as he moves his fingers faster.

"You wouldn't lie to me, would you?" He removes his fingers and I feel like crying from the loss of him.

"You were my first kiss in a very long time," I admit.

"You have no idea how happy that makes me." he slides both fingers back into me, and I turn my head to meet his mouth. He opens for me, his tongue aggressively claiming mine as his fingers work to bring me my desperate release.

I moan loudly against his mouth, "Atlas," I beg.

"Cum for me, Petal," his words push me over and my body twitches against his. He slowly removes his fingers, the bath jets beating loudly with my heavy breaths. "Watching you cum is my new favourite thing. It is better than any high I have ever been on," he kisses my mouth gently. "The things I am going to enjoy doing to you, Petal."

Chapter Ten

Isobel

I wake to Atlas naked beside me, he has kicked away the top blanket, opting for only the white sheet across his body. Even that has fallen to his waist, and I take in the sight of this gorgeous man. His mouth is slightly parted as small breaths escape his lips. Some of his hair has fallen just to the top of both his closed eyes. I resist the urge to trace his features, then I take in some of the different tattoos scattered across his toned body. A gun, a bird, a knife, a snake, the grim reaper, a fern that wraps around his right wrist, so many small tattoos coating his tan skin. Then my eyes follow the different scars. There are two by his collarbone that look different to the rest, but some of them, I am sure, are cigarette burns. I swallow down my pain at the sight of his. So many stories that involve too much suffering. I needed to know more about him, about this man that has moved my still heart.

I can't resist my fingers from tracing the two scars by his collarbone, and his eyes immediately flutter open. I guess being in the army has made him a light sleeper. "Sorry," I whisper.

For a moment, he looks at me like he is the prey, but his eyes quickly change to their relaxed arrogance. "I was shot twice," he says at my fingers still on the two holes.

"What does it feel like?" I gently move my fingers around the scars.

"A burning kind of pain."

"The guy who shot you?"

"Dead, of course," he grins and I can't help but smile back at him; smiling over something quite morbid.

We stayed in the spa until our fingers long turned wrinkly, talking about everything and nothing all at once. Eventually we came back to bed and fell asleep. I realise, as I watch his dangerous smile, and the scars flittering across his skin; that I never would have gone near this man before my cousin destroyed me.

I would have definitely looked his way, as I am sure most women do, but his dead eyes would have been enough for me to never look back. "What is your last name?"

"Christaldi," he moves his hand to my face.

"Atlas Christaldi," I whisper, tasting his name on my lips.

"Isobel Catori," he whispers back.

"You googled me?" I smile.

"Maybe," he rolls on top of me.

"I have to go home," I whisper. His eyes darkening and his jaw clenches slightly. "Why don't you come back with me?"

"If I let you go, how long until you would come back here?"

"You don't own me."

His dangerous smile is back. "Oh Petal, you are mine."

"That doesn't mean you can stop me from seeing Bre and my mum," I say firmly.

"That is why I asked how long you would be," his mouth moves to my neck.

"Don't distract me with that," I attempt to push his head away, but he clasps both of my wrists and holds them firmly above my head.

He sucks and nibbles his way up to my ear. "I do own you Isobel, and if you try to escape me, I will make your life a living hell," he whispers against my ear.

My thighs clench together, I must be truly broken to be turned on by those words. "What would you do?" I whisper.

"No matter how far you run from me, I would find you and I would leave you tied to my bed. No Bre, no Mum, you would be all mine. Or you can tell me you will be back no later than a week and I won't have to resort to such drastic methods."

I gasp, "you would really kidnap me?"

"There is no escaping me Petal, you are mine and I am yours."

"So if you are mine, does that mean the same rules apply? If a girl touches you, I can kill her?"

He laughs at my attempt to sound intimidating. "The thought of another girl touching me is repulsive now Petal, all I see is you."

"I- I won't need a week."

He smirks, "good girl." He begins trailing kisses down my body, settling between my legs, I watch him nervously. He kisses down my thigh, my hand reaching for his hair, before his tongue is swirling over my clit.

"Oh god," I tug at his hair, forgetting how good this feeling is.

"You really do think highly of me, don't you?" His breath on my pussy is enough to beg him for everything.

"Please Atlas," I whisper.

Then his tongue is inside me and my eyes roll to the back of my head. "Jesus Petal, you taste like heaven."

I moan, and rip at his hair, his fingers coming to help his tongue as I realise that this man will have me seeing stars. He lifts my legs over his shoulder so that he can move into me deeper, his tongue sliding down to my ass, I attempt to move away but he pins me to him. "I will fuck all of you," he promises. His tongue moves into my ass, his fingers pumping inside me, and I cry out.

"That feels really good," I moan loudly. The orgasm building in my core, ready to explode throughout my entire body. "Atlas," I cry before the pleasure ripples through me, my body spasms on his face. I don't have a second to catch my breath before he shoves his dick into my mouth, thrusting into me with such force that I close my eyes. He groans loudly before pulling out and spilling his cum over my breasts, his thumb rubbing his warmth over my nipple as his cock jerks the last splutters onto me.

"When you come back, I am going to fuck you until you love me so brutally that I will ruin you for every other man, Petal." He kisses me roughly on the lips before reaching for his discarded clothes.

Love.

For some reason, I didn't think that would be part of this foreign place we are treading. Was I even capable of loving another man again? Was this man before me even capable of such things with the torment so evident across his body?

Fully clothed, he places a hand on my cheek before gently kissing my lips. "Don't make me hunt you," he whispers against my mouth before walking out the door. The weather outside is no longer a violent assault, but a soft promise for a gentle day.

CHAPTER ELEVEN

ISOBEL

Mum's suite is on the top floor, overlooking the ocean. She still does three days a week nursing at the nearby hospital, even though she doesn't need to work ever again if she didn't want to. Her Havanese, Monty is curled in my lap as she brings me a cup of coffee.

"Are you going to tell me the truth?" She asks, handing me the warm mug.

I sigh, not wanting to do this, but also knowing that she deserves it. "I went to Devils Lake." I quickly take a small sip.

"What- why?" She sits on the couch beside me.

"I guess I was trying to understand why Dad went there, and if anyone had seen him."

"Did you take Lewis?"

"Of course," I laugh, knowing how dependant I am becoming of him.

"Di- did you find anything you were looking for?"

I cough, "sort of," I try to hide my blush. "Not about Dad, but I- I met someone..."

"In that short of time?" Mum always loved my ex, Harry, who I dated from sixteen to eighteen. We were high school sweethearts, and we often talked about forever, but Bre caught him fucking our friend Olivia one night at a party. Needless to say, Olivia is no longer our friend, and I broke up with Harry immediately; but Mum always had a sweet spot for him.

"It's very new, but I haven't felt this way before, like ever."

"Oh darling, I always hoped you would find Harry again one day."

"Mum!"

"What?"

"He cheated on me with a friend!"

"Yes, but you were both so young, and he was perfect in every other aspect."

I sigh. Mum has never been treated the way she deserves, so her expectations of men are pretty low. "It won't happen, besides are you even curious about this man I met?"

"Okay, tell me about him."

I realise I shouldn't have said that. "Well, like I said, it is all very new. His name is Atlas."

"That's an interesting name," but her tone is full of judgement.

"And he is a lumberjack," I keep out the fact that he was a Navy Seal.

"How old is he?"

"twenty-six," thankfully, I asked him that in the bath.

"The nice thing about Harry was you were the same age."

"What is the big deal about him being four years older? Probably means he will be too mature to cheat." I can't help but say the words with spite.

"Darling, I'm sorry. I don't want to fight about this, and I am happy for you; I just hope you are taking things slow."

"Of course." *We absolutely aren't.*

"Are you going to be okay doing long distance?"

"Well, I am actually going back there for a while." I move my gaze from hers and pat Monty's head.

"If he is truly worthy of you, then he would come here."

"Mum! You just said you didn't want to fight."

"I don't, but how long are you going for?"

"I don't know, but I can fly you to me whenever you want. Maybe you can meet him." I try to picture my mum and Atlas in the same room, the thought bringing a smile to my lips.

"What is so funny?"

"Nothing, it's hard to explain Mum, but it was like a breath of fresh air being in Devils Lake."

Minus the attempted assault and robbery. "I wrote a lot while I was there..."

Mum places her coffee down on the stone table before grabbing my hand in hers. "Darling, I wish you would talk to me," her eyes are sincere.

"I am talking to you right now, Mum," but I don't remove my hand from hers.

"You know what I mean. I know something happened, something that caused you to stop writing. Caused you to become different...I just wish you felt like you could talk to me about it. I won't judge you. I won't think differently of you, and I can handle anything you tell me." She gently squeezes my hand.

My eyes water, but I hold the tears in. "All you need to know is that I am healing, and Devils Lake is a part of that now. It's nice to get out of the city. There are so many bright trees, and room to breathe; I think you would like it."

"Doubtful, you know how much I love the city now. Isobel...if somebody hurt you, I- I need to know," she whispers.

I suck in a deep breath. "I was hurt, but it is okay now. Please know that things are getting easier."

"Okay," she whispers again. "One day, I hope you feel like you can tell me everything, but I won't keep pushing. Now let's go take Monty for a walk along the beach." At the mention of the word walk, Monty is straight off my lap and heading towards the door where his lead hangs.

<hr />

"Did you tell your mum?" Bre is curling her hair in the bathroom mirror as I finish up my makeup with her bedroom mirror.

"Yeah, she seemed fine about me going, I also told her about Atlas."

"Did she bring up Harry?"

I laugh, dropping my lip gloss away from my mouth. "What do you think?"

"What is it with her and Harry?"

"Who knows? One thing I do know is that Atlas will make her beg for me to take Harry back. She doesn't seem to understand that we haven't spoken in four years. I don't even know anything about him and nor do I want to."

"If you took him back, I would never forgive you. You deserve way more."

"Besides, I never felt the way I do with Atlas about Harry..."

Bre pokes her head through the door. "That serious already!?"

"It's not like serious, it's more intense."

"What kind of intense?"

I can't tell her that he literally threatened to kill anyone that touches me, or that he would kidnap me if I didn't remain his, because all of that sounds unhealthy and insane. "Just the feelings are intense, it's hard to explain."

Maybe Bre wouldn't judge the unhealthy and insane parts of Atlas. Maybe she would understand that I need it. That a part of me will always be on the brink of insanity after what my cousin did. Even though there is a huge part of me that is terrified of Atlas, I also feel extremely safe, safe enough that I would let him do what he pleases with me. "So, is he coming here or?"

"I'm going to go back there for a while, you can come whenever you need." I don't need to add that I will fund her travels. Bre also still works; but I bought her the apartment she lives in, and her Range Rover.

"I think I definitely will, I need to meet this guy. I was worried you would never want a man again," she says gently.

"I also had that same fear."

"Well, since you are going back, we need to go hard tonight," she smiles, plopping on her bed and reaching for her white heels. She is wearing a tight, pale blue dress. Her blonde waves are half pulled away from her face, and her deep blue eyes are coated with a light shimmer. She looks stunning, like she always does. I decide on a shimmering purple dress with shining silver shoes, a high ponytail, with dangly silver earrings. Purple is a favourite colour of mine, I feel it matches my black hair and darker skin, but now all I can think when I see the colour are the purple carnations Atlas seems to enjoy. I wonder if he would like this dress, and a part of me wishes he could see me.

"Lewis!!!!" Bre says as we slide into the back of my Mercedes Benz.

"Hello Bre, Isobel," he smiles.

"Woah, you dropped the formalities, Lewis?" Bre teases.

"I had to beg him," I smile.

"Did you get to meet Atlas?" Bre reaches forward and drapes her arms over his shoulders.

"Seatbelts, and no, I didn't."

"You sure you didn't make him up in your head?" She teases me now.

"Possibly."

"The usual club?"

"You know it, Lewis!" Bre smacks his arm before sliding back and putting her seatbelt on.

For a long time after what my cousin did, I struggled to go out and do the things I enjoy. One of them is dancing to loud music,

I love festivals and different clubs, but eventually Bre dragged me out again. I don't get drunk anymore, nor will I ever do drugs. I am too terrified to ever put myself in a position where I can't control myself again. The feel of the music pulsing through my body is all I ever loved, though; I found that I actually enjoy the night better without getting drunk.

"Do you want to come in with us?" I ask Lewis.

"Maybe another time," he smiles as the noise from the club filters into the car.

"Okay, I'll message you."

"Be safe, you two."

"Always Lewis!" Bre winks at him before following me out. One of the best things about being a successful author is that I am extremely rich without the fame. I mean, some fans will recognise me and ask for an autograph, but mainly people just know the actors from my stories. It is a privilege to still be able to do everything relatively normal without the fear of paparazzi or people swarming me.

We dodge the line, going straight into our VIP section. Bre likes to drink a lot before we head onto the dancefloor, and I will have one or two with her. Our section overlooks the dancers and another bar below. I pull my phone out and notice a message from an unknown number.

Remember my promise, Petal.

I suck in a breath before quickly looking around the club.

Are you here?

I stare at my phone screen until he replies, my heart beating desperately in my chest.

> **I turned on your location. If you turn it off, you will be punished.**

Sadness fills me, I was excited thinking he would see me in this dress, that I could kiss him on the dancefloor, and Bre could meet him.

"What is it?" Bre asks.

"Hmm?"

"You look like you have seen a ghost."

"Oh no, it's nothing, just a message from Atlas." He turned my location on and got my number, probably when I fell asleep.

"Please tell me he isn't one of those controlling guys that won't let you dance with me," she rolls her eyes.

"No, he just wants to make sure I get home safe," I lie.

"Well, that is just sweet," she sips at her vodka cocktail. "So, are you going to tell me what has changed with you and Lewis?"

"We haven't changed that much," I reach for my own cocktail.

"He isn't as shy, and you both seem like best friends now, which is impossible, of course, because I am your best friend."

I laugh as she bats her eyelashes dramatically at me. "I may have accidentally fallen asleep at Atlas's one night and forgot to tell him. He spent the whole night thinking I was dead, so I took him out for dinner the next night, and now we are friends."

"You slept at Atlas's!? Does that mean?"

"No- we didn't, but we did other things."

She smiles wickedly at me. "What things?"

"Come on Bre, we aren't in high school anymore. I don't need to tell you what we did." This time, I roll my eyes at her.

"Umm, when it has been over a year since you have even looked at a guy, I think I am allowed some details! Also, do you have a picture of him?"

"No, I didn't ask about social media and all that," I wave my hand. I doubt Atlas was the sort of guy that even has any socials, I only have socials for my author accounts.

"Give me something Iz!"

"Okay, he has tattoos," her eyebrows raise at that. "Dark blonde hair with green eyes, and he cuts wood for a living."

"So he is ripped?"

"You could definitely say that," I smile sweetly.

She claps her hands excitedly. "And his dick?" She moves closer with anticipation. I shrug, smiling into my drink.

"Come on, you need to at least give me that detail!"

I lean in close, so that no one will be able to hear, not that they could with the loud music. "The kind that will split me in half."

She squeals in delight. "Jesus Iz, he sounds perfect!"

"I think he is perfect for me, for what I need now."

"Hello ladies," we both look up at two men sliding into our booth. An arm is draped over my shoulder to try to bring me closer, but I move away from his touch.

"I'm taken," I say firmly. The guy with dark hair and a lazy grin would definitely be considered handsome, but Atlas is the only man to bring that wanting from my soul.

"No way a man is letting a pretty girl like you out of his sight," his smirk grows and I feel repulsed by him.

"My man trusts me." I glance over to Bre, who is sizing her guy up, going through her mental list of whether this guy is worth her time.

He reaches for a strand of my hair and I flinch away from his touch. "I am going to get us all some drinks," he chuckles before standing.

"I don't want drinks," I say firmly again.

"Yeah piss off, it's girls' night," Bre says.

The two boys head towards the bar, and I hope that they don't come back. "Should we go dance?"

"Yes!" Bre skulls her drink and I leave the rest of mine on the table, knowing that I won't be coming back to it.

I love dancing until my hair sticks to my neck from sweat, until the beat from the music feels like it has replaced the beating inside me. Before Atlas, this is the only way I could feel anything move my heart, feel any kind of rush or high. Bre lets a couple of guys grind up against her, but I make my movements unapproachable, as I always do now. It doesn't stop one guy from pulling me to him, his body attempting to grind against mine as I push him away, he pulls me back tighter. So I turn and push at his chest with all my might, shoving him away with anger.

I watch as his eyes flash with rage, he grabs my mouth forcefully. "Tease!" He yells, and before I have time to respond, Bre has jumped on his back, smashing her fist into his head. He throws her to the ground, just as security reach us and drag him away.

"Bre!" I scream and rush for her, but she is laughing as I haul her up.

"What a piece of shit!"

I smile at her, "you are nuts, you know that?"

"Are you done, or do you want to keep dancing?" She yells over the music.

"I will message Lewis."

We begin walking away from the dancefloor. "I need pizza!"

"Mmm, and a shake," she giggles, linking her arm with mine as we leave the club.

CHAPTER TWELVE

ATLAS

I take a bite of my turkey roll as I watch where Isobel is heading, back to her mums by the looks of it. It was harder than I thought seeing her in that purple dress, and not fucking her senseless in front of every man that looked her way. The problem with giving in to that urge would be the amount of men I would have to murder after they saw her pretty face cum from my dick. I'm hard just thinking about that tight dress hugging her curves as she went into her own world on the dancefloor.

It's like she knows what purple does to me. That second night she wore a purple knit at the bar was all the sign I needed.

But watching her was also fascinating, especially when I messaged her and she got her hopes up looking around for me. She misses me, I could see that clearly last night. She is smart too, whether she realises she is doing it or not, she covers her drink so that no one can chuck a pill in quickly, she also didn't get drunk, maybe a lot of that has to do with what her cousin did to her.

When I saw where her location went to last night, I had to follow, and although I have much bigger things to be addressing;

I couldn't not make sure she was safe. Then that fuckhead put his arm around her, and even after she immediately moved from him, he still tried to reach for her hair. Isobel was such a good girl, but he was persistent. I'm a reasonable man. I can understand a guy trying, but the second they don't walk away with the first no; is when I need to teach them a lesson.

I lured him to the bathroom, telling him I had something he could use to slip into the pretty girl's drinks. The sick fuck was easily persuaded with that one, furthering my need to punish him. I broke his nose with a quick jab, the blood spilling out faster than he could stop it. Then I broke the hand he used to touch her, touch her even though she moved away the first time. I left him unconscious on the floor after smashing his head against the sink.

Which brings me to the next manner of issues. The piece of shit that practically forced himself onto her while she was dancing. I smile as I remember Bre jumping onto his back, beating him with all her strength; she is a firecracker. I most definitely approve of her as Isobel's best friend. I am well and truly obsessed with my Petal. I cannot stop thinking of my blood coating her perfect cunt, of the way her face looks when she comes from my fingers and mouth. I need all of her, in every way conceivable.

"Please!" A voice calls out.

I finish up my sandwich, chucking the paper bag in the bin before dusting off my hands on my jeans. Back to business, I guess.

"Please, just tell me what you want!"

I walk out into the open warehouse that has been abandoned, to where I have left the forceful piece of shit tied up. After he was kicked out by security, I couldn't let what he did slide. He wouldn't have stopped if there was no one to pull him away, and I know Isobel isn't the first girl he has pulled that crap on; I also know she won't be the last.

He begins shaking as I slowly walk up to him. "What the fuck do you want, man? I've never met you in my life."

"No, but I know one of the girls you decided to harass."

His face goes even paler, so I was right. He has done much worse to other women. "I am here to deliver your punishment."

"I- I have money. I can get you whatever you want," he pleads.

"What I want is for your hands to never touch another woman." I smile darkly at him.

"Done. I swear to you I will become a monk if you just let me go," his eyes holding so much terror as I pick up the butcher's cleaver I stole.

The begging and pleading only excites me further. I enjoy hurting men that hurt others, especially the kind that prey on the weak. "You see- Ahh, what was your name again?"

"Evan," he tries to keep his tone from wavering.

"Yes Evan, the thing is you can give me your word all you want, but I don't actually believe you," my smile grows as I spin the cleaver around.

"P-please," he wets himself.

"How many girls begged you, the way you are begging me? Did you ever stop Evan?"

He begins crying; the snot leaking out his nose in a humiliating way. In one clean swipe, I bring the blade down over one of his hands, cutting it clean off. His screams fill the warehouse. "You motherfucker!!"

"I was wondering when you would get mad," I smile before cutting the other hand off.

He screams louder this time, "PLEASE!" He begs me to stop. His head drops low to his chest as he fights against the pain from his severed hands.

"Did you ever think to ask yourself one simple question..." I taunt.

"W-what?" He sobs.

"Why I'm not wearing a mask? Could have saved yourself a lot of begging." I swing the cleaver into his throat, wedging it deep as his eyes stop moving and his head slumps to the side.

Now for my least favourite bit, discarding the body, and then on to more pressing matters.

CHAPTER THIRTEEN

ISOBEL

After spending a couple of days with Mum, and my last one with Bre, I am well and truly missing Atlas now. I debated sending him a dozen messages, sometimes even starting the text before deleting it; but I don't want to come across as too strong. Not that I think it will matter, he is the most intense man I have ever met, already talking about me falling in love with him.

"Let me know when you want me to come, okay?" Bre helps pack two large suitcases for me, taking more than I did last time.

"I will probably want you after the first day," I smile as I tuck in some more lacy lingerie. Bre doesn't comment, she knows I wear that kind of underwear all the time, I just enjoy feeling pretty.

"Do you think you will message him to let him know you are coming back?" She folds another coat in.

"Maybe." I don't tell Bre that I'm sure Atlas will be tracking my location to the airport.

"Surprises are fun," she shrugs. "It might be nice for Lewis to have a break from me, I think he is getting tired of my drunken antics."

"He's not as prim and proper as you think, Bre," I smile as I remember the dinner we had together where he shocked the living shit out of me.

"What do you mean?"

"Keep annoying him and you might find out."

"I love stirring him up and watching him go all shy," she flops onto my bed.

"I know," I grin.

"I'm glad that you picked him," she stares up at my ceiling.

"Me too," I admit.

"I feel safe with him, like he would never take advantage of us in any way."

"He wouldn't." I wonder if Lewis would approve of Atlas after coming from a toxic relationship. I'm not stupid enough to believe Atlas and I aren't toxic. He has already expressed his love of control, of pushing boundaries and threatening to punish me. But he can also be so gentle, stroking my face and hair, soothing me through my trauma. In the brief time we have had together, it almost feels like he understands what I need more than I do.

Maybe it was never really about finding out what happened to my father. Maybe it was always about finding Atlas.

"How is your mum going with you, leaving again?"

"She seems okay, I steered it in the direction that Devils Lake is helping me to write again." Which isn't a total lie.

She rolls over to watch me as I finish up my packing. "Do you think you will ever tell her?" She asks gently.

My hands freeze what they are doing, as I steady the fear rising in my breaths. "I think it would destroy her," I whisper.

"I think your mum would do what needs to be done to put him away," she counters.

"Then I would have to see him again, and on top of all that it was a year ago and I was so drunk. There will never be enough evidence to put myself through everything."

"Don't you want him punished?"

"Of course, I have murdered him thousands of times in my mind," I offer her a small smile.

"That is not the same and you know it."

I sigh, "why are you bringing this up?"

"I just think that more support couldn't hurt, and your mum would do anything for you."

"One day, maybe," I zip up my suitcase and she comes to stand beside me; wrapping her arms around my body tightly.

"I love you Iz, you are such a strong person."

"I love you," I whisper, sniffing away a couple of tears.

Bre walks me out to where Lewis is waiting, her range rover is parked in my driveway and Lewis is tucked behind. He quickly gets out to load my bags, offering us both a warm smile. "You going to miss me, Lewis?" Bre taunts with raised eyebrows.

"Extremely so," he closes the trunk.

"Really?" She leans into him slightly, trying to bring on that blush and shyness.

"Yes, kind of like how a dog misses fleas," he smiles sweetly.

Bre steps back in shock. "So you won't miss me at all and you compare me to a flea?"

I give her a look that says I told you so, you poked the bear one too many times. He winks before getting into the driver's seat. "Well, that was rude," she comes and gives me one last hug.

"I did warn you," I hold her hands in mine.

"He just caught me off guard, I need to up my game," she smiles mischievously.

"Whatever you say, I will see you soon Bre."

She smiles at me, "make sure to message me when you land."

As Lewis and I wait at our gate for boarding, my phone vibrates. I saved his number when he messaged me at the nightclub, my heart pounds seeing his name light up my screen.

> I'll be seeing you soon, Petal.

My hand hovers over the keys, feeling a nervous electricity.

> I'm a little nervous.

I didn't know whether admitting that was the right thing to do, I stare at the screen; desperate for his reply.

> You should be.

CHAPTER FOURTEEN

ISOBEL

"Y ou sure you don't want to just stay at The Lodge tonight? It's already getting late." Lewis opens the door for me, and I slide into the back of the car with my overnight bag.

"I need to see him." I don't know if that sounds pathetic, but at this point, I don't care. I also know that if I don't go to him, he will come to The Lodge within the hour.

Lewis smiles as he shuts my door. "My phone will be on loud if you need me to get you, but I will just assume you don't want to be picked up this time."

My cheeks warm, and I avoid his gaze in the review mirror. "Thank you, Lewis."

I fidget with my small gold ring as Lewis remembers the way to Atlas's house, he wants me nervous, and scared. Part of him gets off on my fear, and a part of me gets off on being frightened. In a sick and twisted way, we really are perfect for each other.

The car slows down as we pull into the trailer park, heading for the one with handcrafted wood that lines every inch. The porch light is on, and standing at the top of the small staircase is Atlas.

He has his arms crossed as he leans his shoulder against the railing. My hands feel clammy as I attempt to stop my fidgeting.

"Jesus Christ," Lewis breathes.

"I know," I whisper.

"I want one."

I laugh, Lewis distracting my terrified heart as I grab my bag. "Maybe you should go out tonight, see if you can find your own lumberjack?" I raise my eyebrows.

"Don't tempt me Isobel, you kids have fun."

"I'm one year younger than you, and he's older," I point to the porch.

He reaches for my hand just as my other one grabs the door handle. "My phone is on loud," he reminds me.

"Thank you, I will message you tomorrow, but please just have the night off, okay?"

He smiles, "goodnight."

"Night," I smile as the freezing night air encompasses my body. How the shit is Atlas just standing up there in a shirt? I can see the smoke leaving his chimney, relief floods through me, knowing I will be warm soon enough.

In more ways than one.

My shoes crunch as I walk through the snow to him, my hands shaking not just from the cold. I climb the four steps, "hey," I whisper.

He is smirking down at me. "Hello," he takes my bag and then stretches out his arm for me to head inside. He closes the door behind me, leaving my bag on the ground as I look around his inviting home. Before I have time to react, he slams me against the wall; I gasp out from the contact. He swallows my breath with his mouth, pushing his entire body into me as his hand wraps around my throat. I kiss him greedily, missing the feel of his body against mine, missing the feel of his power. "Did you miss me, Petal?" He pants against my mouth.

"Yes." I smash my lips back against his, my nerves dissipating from the way he ignites me. Coating my entire body with small sparks that flicker around his space, his own fire holding me in a fervent grip.

He lifts me, carrying me to his bed, his mouth never leaving mine as his desperation soaks into me. He stands me before the bed, only breaking away from my lips to remove my clothing, I fumble with his; needing to feel his naked body against mine.

Sliding onto the bed, the nerves creep back in. I had forgotten just how huge he is. I have never had his size inside me, and now with my issues down there...this feels impossible. "Atlas..." I breathe nervously, scooting myself further away from him.

"We will make it fit Petal," he rips my legs back towards him, as he crawls between me.

His mouth moving from my lips, down to my neck before reaching my nipples. He teases one with his fingers and the other with his mouth. "Atlas," I moan. He continues his trailing lower, and as his tongue moves inside me, I cry out.

He spits onto my entrance, then he kneels between my open legs, and spits onto his cock, rubbing it around for extra lubricant, before he brings the tip of it back to my open thighs. As he begins to push inside me, I clutch at the sheets. I start shaking my head back and forth, there is absolutely no way this is fitting. "Hey," he grabs my jaw firmly to stop me from moving my protesting head. "Hold onto me, dig your nails into my skin and draw as much blood as you need, because I am not stopping now Petal." I do what he says, placing my hands on his shoulders, and with each slow movement he pushes into me, I dig my nails in deeper to him. "Fuck, I'm nearly all the way in."

I watch the pleasure cover his face as tears build at the corners of my eyes. I breathe as I dig my nails deeper into his skin. With one last slow thrust, he settles into me. He leans down and kisses each tear away. "You are doing so well Petal," slowly he begins to move. "I have never felt a pussy so tight, you are made for me," he groans as he pulls out and then pushes all the way back in. "I-I can't keep going slow," he moans, and my own sound moves from my lips at the sight of him losing himself inside me.

"I can handle it," I pant.

He smiles, "that's my good girl," and then he fucks me hard and fast. I scream out, the pain mixing with pleasure as he fills me so completely that I will be forever empty without him. "I need you to cum baby, because you are so fucking tight and I can't hold out much longer." He lifts one of my legs over his shoulder, groaning as it moves him even deeper.

"Atlas," I moan loudly. "I'm going to-" My words cut off as the pressure explodes throughout me, the sparks morphing into fireworks as I erupt beneath him. He follows me, his groans growing heavy as he spills himself inside me, thrusting a few more times as he pushes his cum deeper. "I can feel you," I murmur in disbelief.

"I have been saving all my cum for you Petal," he lays onto me, his chest heaving against my own. Slowly he begins to withdraw from me, I wince from the pain and from the loss of him.

He kisses every inch of my face, showing me how proud he is of me, before he gets up and turns from the bed. "Atlas!" I gasp as I see his back- see what I have done to him. He is covered in deep scratches, most bleeding and some already beginning to bruise. He brings back a wet towel, wiping the warmth of it between my legs to clean me, his touch now is so gentle from the man that claimed me before. "I'm so sorry," I whisper.

"Don't ever apologise for making me bleed. I have already told you I will bleed whenever you need me to. You are never to be alone in your pain again, when you hurt, I hurt as well. Is that clear?" I nod my head, swallowing my shock within myself. "Answer me."

"Yes, we will hurt together," I whisper.

"Always together Petal, because there is no world where we can be apart now."

Chapter Fifteen

Atlas

My Petal fell asleep shortly after I held her tight, but I couldn't follow her. I stare at her peaceful face, the flames from my wood heater lighting up her perfect features. I have never been so obsessed in my life. I have been in a relationship before, but never have I felt the suffocating hold of love. It is so consuming that the thought of not having her is impossible. I would burn the world to the ground if someone took her from me, and if she ran... If she ran from me, there would be no place she could go that would be far enough. I would tear apart the entire fucking world to find her.

I would hold her and fuck her until she loved me just as fiercely. Even if I have to force her feelings, she will not be able to survive without me. There is nothing I wouldn't do to keep her as mine, and as I brush the hair back from her face, she smiles in her sleep for me.

My touch makes her happy, and it's the most beautiful thing I have ever witnessed. That, and the face she makes when she comes. It's fucking intoxicating watching her come undone for me, the noises she makes are like the gates of heaven opening. Isobel Catori is the closest thing to heaven I will ever get to feel, and now that I have my foot through the threshold, I will never leave. I would sooner drag her down to hell with me than let her go.

I think of my cum being inside her, the tingles that moved through my stomach at the thought of her on no birth control. I know that she is on the pill, from when I searched her bags the last time she fell asleep before me. But I picture her pregnant with my child, she could never escape me then.

The unhinged thought of swapping the pills for fake ones has me hard again. I debate pushing inside her, using my cum as lube this time. The thrill I would get from watching the fear coat her face as she would wake to find my cock fucking her. Fear that would quickly turn to pleasure as I drive myself into her over and over again.

I restrain myself, knowing how sore she would be; my back and her pussy need a little break. I want her healed only so I can ruin her again, only so that she can be so full of my cum, it is our version of making her wet.

I rest my hand against her cheek, and she moves closer to me, nuzzling her head against mine. Slowly my eyes grow heavy, slowly, I find peace with her beside me.

We will ruin each other, Petal.

I wake to my alarm buzzing loudly beside me, and reach quickly to turn it off as Isobel stretches her hands above her head. "Mmm," she sighs. I kiss her lightly on the lips before getting out of bed. "Where are you going?" Her eyes work at staying open.

I smile at how adorable she is. "I have work baby," I quickly shove on my clothing as her smile moves to a frown. "Stay here and write, there's food in the fridge. I will be back later and I expect you to be here."

She chuckles, her eyes closing once more. "Always so bossy," she smiles.

"That wasn't a 'yes Atlas, I will be here when you get back'," I push firmly.

She opens her eyes and I see the dance of disobedience flickering there, "aye, aye Captain," she gives me a salute with a grin now stretching her face.

I lean down on my bed, and whisper into her ear, "I will punish you when I get home." I breathe heavily before biting her lobe, her whole body squirming. "And if you disobey that order, I will fuck you until you're too bruised to run away from me."

I watch as she swallows down her fear.

I smile darkly, "don't you dare touch yourself while I am gone Petal, your orgasms belong to me now."

CHAPTER SIXTEEN

ISOBEL

Eventually, after the desire along my skin settles, I fall back to sleep. I don't touch myself, not knowing how he would possibly know if I have, and although a part of me wanted to defy him; I don't. Mainly because there is no way my fingers will compare to his touch now, so even if I did disobey him, I wouldn't feel satisfied without him.

A wake to the sun up, with snow gently falling outside and the fire crackling. Atlas must have opened the flue up before he left. I smile at his thoughtfulness, at the man who both terrifies me and looks out for me. I place the coffeepot on top of the fire before having a soothing shower, then I stock up the woodpile for today and tonight. I make myself eggs on toast, clean up the dishes I use before settling back into his bed with my laptop. I send Lewis a message that I will be staying here today and that he can go hunt down his own lumberjack.

Maybe I already found him last night.

I laugh at his response, I hope he never wants to work for someone else; my heart couldn't handle losing him now. I start the process of sorting through emails, answering some fans and also sending off the beginnings of my new work to my agent. Who will then send it to our editor, and as I bring my story up to continue writing, my phone rings.

"Hi Mum," I answer enthusiastically.

"Isobel, you are in a good mood," her tone is happy.

"Yes, I just started writing; how are you?"

"Good darling, I was just wondering if you have heard from your cousin?"

The blood drains from my face at the mention of him. I cough to hide my discomfort. "No Mum, why is that?"

"Well, your uncle rang me and asked if either of us have heard from him because he is missing."

Panic rises in my gut. Could he possibly be following me? "No, you know I don't really talk to them and I haven't seen them for a while now."

"I know, that's what I thought," she pauses for a moment. "Do you think maybe they got caught up in something? Your father and him, I mean...like maybe a gang?" She whispers the last word, like saying the word gang is going to make one jump out and start beating us.

"I mean...I guess anything is possible." Maybe they are all caught up in something dodgy, that thought is better than thinking he is stalking me to Devils Lake. I wish Atlas would come home now. The rational side of my brain tells me that he would have no way of knowing where I am.

"So, when do I get to meet him?" Mum asks, changing the subject.

"When I can be confident you won't compare him to Harry."

"I would never do that to his face, darling."

I sigh and she laughs, "if he makes you happy, I want to meet him."

"Thank you Mum, but it is still early, so maybe give it a little longer yet."

"Okay, well, I will let you get back to your writing; I love you Isobel."

"Love you too, Mum."

The hours move by as I lose myself within my story, my fingers constantly tapping my keys as everything seems to fall into place as I write. I only stop to start cooking dinner, a creamy pasta that I make from ingredients in his house. Just as I turn the stove off, the door opens.

Atlas walks inside, hanging up his bag and shrugging off his coat. His hair is lined with tiny specs of snow, and parts of his face and arms are covered with smudges of dirt.

He looks so fucking hot.

I rush to him, jumping into his arms and wrapping my legs around his waist. "I could get used to coming home to this," he breathes me in as I nuzzle into his neck. "Are you wearing my shirt?"

"Yes, you smell like the forest," I lick up his neck.

He cups my ass and groans, "no underwear, Petal?" I giggle before kissing him. "You wouldn't be trying to get out of your punishment, would you?"

"Never," I bat my eyelashes innocently. "I- I don't like it when you leave..." I say hesitantly.

His eyes soften at my words, like he is shocked about how I am feeling. "Whatever I have left inside here," he points to his heart, "is yours Petal. And if you ever go, I will be nothing but hollow inside. Don't you ever fucking leave me, baby." His eyes hold more love as he looks into mine, more than I have ever seen before.

"I won't," I promise, and then I kiss him hard; moaning against his lips as his fingers dig into my ass.

He places me on his bed, pushing his shirt up to free my breasts. Then he spits on his fingers as he roughly spreads my legs apart with his other hand. "I have been thinking about your tight little pussy all day," he rubs his spit around before slipping a finger inside.

"I have been thinking about this all day," I breathe.

He gives me a cocky smile. "Really Petal? One time and you are already obsessed?"

I moan as he adds another finger, "Atlas," I pant. Desperate for the release that only he can bring me. "I'm going to-"

Just as I feel the pressure build, he withdraws his fingers and smacks my clit. I gasp out in complete shock. "Do you think you deserve to cum?" He moves his fingers back inside me, bringing me so close to the edge before he removes them again.

I whimper, "is this my punishment?"

He leans down, bringing his lips to my ear. "Aye, aye captain," he whispers.

I squirm as he moves his fingers back into me, and as I feel close, I reach down to hold his fingers inside me. He stills his movements, and with his free hand, he roughly grabs my throat, pushing my head hard into his mattress. "I say when your punishment is over," he growls out and I let go of his hand only to grab at the one squeezing my throat. The darkness begins taking my vision. "Do you enjoy the little stars I bring you, Petal?"

He releases his grip, but leaves his hand on my throat as I choke in air to my lungs. "Please," I cough.

"Please what?" He smirks.

I control my ragged breathing as I stare him down, not wavering from the fear he installs. "Fuck me until the stars come for us both."

He begins unbuckling his belt, and I hide my smile, the fear of him changing his mind hanging in the air. "On all fours Petal."

I do what he asks and turn around on my hands and knees. He spanks me as he pushes his cock against me, showing me how hard he is for me. "When you cum Petal, remember only I can give you this. You. Are. Mine." He pushes inside me slowly, letting me adjust to the feel of him. "Jesus, it's like fucking a virgin every time with you."

"It's so deep," I moan out. I go to clutch at the bedding but he rips both of my arms behind me, holding them in place as my face hits the sheets. He fucks me rough and hard, my screams soon echoing across his trailer, and as my body finishes shuttering from my orgasm, he rips me up by my hair; my back resting against his chest. "Your pleasure belongs to me, your pain belongs to me, your happiness and your fear belong to me, Petal," he says against my mouth. "I. Own. You." He groans as our mouths collide, my tongue darting aggressively for his. He thrusts violently a couple more times before he fills me with his cum, his breath hot against mine as his fingers dig at the flesh underneath my breast.

We both fall to the bed, desperate pants calming our insatiable bodies. "Atlas?"

"Yeah baby?" He strokes my hair while staring into my eyes.

"Why do you call me Petal?"

"Because you are beautiful and delicate, and extremely easy to pull apart."

I suck in a breath, "and you want to pull me apart?"

He smiles, "only so I can put you back together."

Chapter Seventen

Atlas

Coming home to her cooking in nothing but my shirt stirred something primal inside me. Something like a better future floated through my mind. One where Isobel is home to greet me, one where happiness thrives from her smile. The excitement that lit up her face when I came home pulled at my dead heart. She is already falling for me and it is fucking consuming the way she needs me.

Her wobbly legs walk back to the stove to serve our dinner up, and I can't help the smirk that comes from watching her. "Oh no," she says as she spoons the pasta into a bowl.

"Yes Petal?"

She goes a delicious shade of pink. "Your cum is falling out," she attempts to shut her legs together.

I walk over to her, "be a good girl and clean it up baby," my cock grows hard as I watch her eyes go wide. She moves her hand between her thighs, then slowly brings the cum to her mouth; sucking on her fingers as she watches me. "How does it taste?" My breath catching as she moans and her eyes close, savouring my taste. Then she reaches between her legs again, bringing my cum to my lips, I open my mouth and suck myself from her fingers.

"See how incredible you taste," she whispers.

I am a fucking goner.

I lift her, placing her onto the counter as I stand between her legs. "You are fucking perfect," I push inside her once more, my cum providing plenty of lubrication.

"Atlas," she wraps her legs tighter around my waist, bringing me even deeper.

Nothing has ever felt as perfect as her cunt, I feel like I can't see or think straight when I am inside her. "Look at your pussy swallowing my cock," she drops her head down to watch between us, her moans growing heavier as I slowly pull out of her, only to slam myself back in.

"Atlas- I love you," she pants.

I grab her face between both my hands, "say that again Petal," stilling my movements inside her.

"I love you," tears brush the corners of her eyes.

I smile, my mouth finding hers as I start to slowly thrust again, her moans getting caught against my lips. "I fucking love you. I will never stop loving you, Isobel."

A tear falls down her cheek, but I brush it away. "Until death?"

"Petal, not even death will part us, I will follow you wherever you go; God himself couldn't keep me from you."

She sobs at my words, her lips lightly brushing mine as I fuck her harder. Needing to see the stars our bodies bring together.

"Atlas," she cries out as her pussy tightens even harder around me, the spasms of her orgasm pushing me to finish.

"Fuck baby," I groan as I spill my cum into her, my favourite place to finish.

We rest our foreheads against each other as our bodies come back down from the sky. "Should we eat dinner?"

I laugh, "if I am going to fuck you again tonight, then we definitely should."

Her wide eyes cause me to chuckle, I pick her up and carry her to my small table, sitting her down with a quick kiss on her head. Then I finish dishing up the pasta and bring it over for her. "Should I re-heat it?"

"I'm too hungry to care at this point," placing the lukewarm pasta into my mouth, I hum my appreciation. "Not just a pretty face?"

She shrugs, "I have my talents," she smiles.

"Thought you would have your own chef," I tease.

"You know I grew up on a reservation, right? In a trailer far less nice than this," she gestures around my home with her fork. "Maybe your google stalking isn't up to scratch?" She raises her eyebrows.

"I know you did baby," I say gently. "I mean now."

She shrugs again. "I don't really like people in my house. It took a lot to even hire Lewis, but my life would be terrible without him now."

We finish dinner, then have a shower together, my dick wanting to take her again in there; but she dropped to her knees and sucked me dry. Her wet hair bunched in my fingers as I fucked her mouth, not stopping when she choked; not stopping until my cum slid down her throat and she smiled up at me breathless.

Those big dark eyes will surely be my undoing. The way they stare at the blackness of my soul and still find something worth loving. We lay in bed together, I am in nothing but my underwear, and she is in nothing but another one of my shirts, my new favourite outfit on her.

Her fingers lightly trace the different scars stretching across my torso, something I have never let anyone do before. And although it makes my hands clammy, and my chest thump, I know that I need to let her. She has told me her scars; it is only fair to let her caress mine. "Tell me…" she whispers. "What happened to you, all this suffering…" Her voice laced with disbelief.

"It's not worth your pain Petal," I say simply.

She sits up, looking into my eyes that have gone to a place where living is questionable. "We hurt together, remember?"

Fucking hell, there is no survival without this woman now. "Don't use my words against me," I smile at her, stroking her hair to bring her head back against my chest. "My mum became a crack addict, she had many different boyfriends, most of which I can't remember; but two stood out."

"Your father?" She whispers.

"I never knew him, Mum never spoke of who he was, and I'm not even sure if she knew." She wraps her arms around me tighter, her head resting on top of my heart. "One of these boyfriends enjoyed physically hurting me, leaving different marks for no reason at all. It started off as punishment when I did something wrong, but it eventually turned into 'well I don't have an ashtray, so Atlas's skin will do.'" She sucks in a deep breath, my pain flowing into her with an ease I didn't know would be possible. "The other one was much worse," my voice becomes dark and cold as Isobel seemingly still holds her breath. "He would sneak into my room each night, force me onto my knees and shove his tiny cock down my throat." Isobel lets her gasp be drowned out by a sob. She does her best to let her tears silently fall to my chest, her fingers digging into my skin as she holds me tighter.

"How old were you?" She asks, her tone wavering with sadness.

"Between the both of them, it was six till fourteen."

"Wh-why didn't your mum do anything?" Her tone has moved to anger.

"They hurt her too, but mum was getting too far gone by this point; doing anything for her next hit. They often had their friends come over; she would let them all fuck her if it would give her some smack."

"Why you will never kneel for anyone..." she says, more to herself.

"Yes Petal," I confirm her speaking thoughts.

"Where are they now?" Her voice has gone dark and my dick stirs at her tone.

"Dead. The one that left these marks was shot down by some cops after running from them."

"The other one?" Her voice remains cold, like she is debating all the ways she will hurt him. I grow hard, needing to bring her cold voice back to soft moans.

"I cut his tiny dick off, forced him to swallow it; and then let him bleed out while he begged me for mercy."

She remains silent for a moment; I roll over so that she is beneath me. "That's psychopathic," but a tiny smile tugs at the side of her mouth.

"Yes, but you already knew that about me; didn't you Petal?" I move myself between her legs, nipping and kissing down her thigh. I slide two fingers covered in my spit inside her. Her moans are the most heavenly sounds, sounds that I need to hear everyday now. "You like it, don't you? That you let a psychopath between your pretty legs?" She moans louder, and I sink my teeth into the inside of her thigh; tasting her sweet metallic blood. "Answer me."

Her leg shakes from the pain and pleasure. "Yes," she cries out as my tongue swipes her clit and I groan against her as she tugs at my hair.

"You might want to tug harder," I spit on her ass, her moans quietening as anticipation catches her quick breaths. I slide one finger into her tight ass, and she rips at my hair in response. "Has anyone ever fucked you here, Petal?"

I look up at her, and she shakes her head. "No," she whispers.

I smile at the slight fear flickering across her face. "I will have you begging me to fuck your ass so hard, you won't know which you will prefer," and then I add another finger as her head drops back to the pillow.

"It hurts a little," she whispers.

"Rip my hair as hard as you need," then my tongue moves from her pussy to her clit as my fingers fuck her tiny ass.

"Why does this feel so good?" She moans, thrusting her hips into my face to bring all of me deeper. "Oh Atlas!" Her legs quiver around my head as I slow my movements.

"Fucking perfect," I kiss her cunt before sliding my body up hers, kissing her lips as her eyes fall heavy. "My Petal is so good to me," I whisper against her head, pulling her into the nook of my arm; tracing my fingers lightly along her skin.

I wake to my alarm, Isobel's eyes hardly stirring as I get ready. I have exhausted her; I smile as I kiss her goodbye. The more I tire her, the less likely she will ever run away. Lewis is parked in the same spot as last night. I sigh, my breath fogging with the freezing air. Knocking on his car window, he jolts awake.

Winding it down as he stretches out his arms. "Probably not a good idea to leave your car running all night," I offer.

"Well, it's either that or I freeze to death," his throat is dry.

"Why don't you stay at The Lodge?"

"In case she needs me," he looks at me with no fear. "You better not hurt her."

I rip his face against the car door, smashing the side of his head. He jumps out of the car, shaking his angry head. "Fuck was that for!?"

"Fight me Lewis, if you are so desperate to protect her," I smirk.

"Fuck is wrong with you," he swings a jab for me, but I dodge his punch.

The next time he swings, I grab his fist. "I like you Lewis."

His confused eyes search mine. "Why?"

"Anyone willing to fight me in order to protect a friend is a good man." He drops his hand from mine. "Go get some rest, she is always safe with me."

CHAPTER EIGHTEEN

ISOBEL

I take in my reflection in Atlas's bathroom. There is bruising around my neck, and a deep purple bruise on the inside of my thigh, Atlas's teeth marks making up the darker tones. I trace the markings lightly with my fingers, my eyes moving to my face, to the skin that is glowing and to the eyes that look alive. I smile, my heart racing at the discolouring from Atlas's work.

I should feel sick.

I should feel terror and pain, disgust even.

Instead, I want more.

More colours, more exhilaration, more Atlas.

My body, mind and heart are so wholly alive with him. He has consumed me fully, and the thought that he could do pretty much whatever he wanted to me, doesn't scare me; it thrills me.

I would gladly go to the depths of every dark part of his mind, and instead of running; I would ask him if we could fall deeper.

Here I am, in this dark and twisted kind of love; and all I see is light. The light in his pale green eyes, the light in the way he smiles at me, a smile I imagine not many see. The light in the sparks we create with our bodies, the light that explodes from the words; *I love you*. Every ounce of his darkness can encompass me, because it is his darkness that has me seeing so clearly.

The money and the readers couldn't save me, my mother or Bre couldn't either, only him. Only Atlas could bring me back to life with fear, excitement, and passion. Leaving him would mean a death sentence for me, for any chance at feeling anything other than numb. I decided a long time ago that a part of me was forever lost the night my cousin raped me, the chance of me loving again were so slim; and the chance for that love to be conventional was impossible. The warped and toxic love that we have is my only shot at happiness.

I need Atlas.

He is greater than any therapy, any drug, greater than anything that could bring me back. When I think back to Harry, before my cousin abused me, if he had left marks on my skin, I would have run so far. I would have let Bre unleash all her wrath upon him and then walked straight to the cops to press charges. Timing is this ironic force, much bigger than I could ever comprehend. Time knew that I could never handle Atlas before my cousin. She waited patiently for a part in our lives where our love could survive.

I shower, washing my hair and applying a small amount of makeup, before texting Lewis to come pick me up. I wear my purple knit that hides most of my neck and step outside into the crunching snow where Lewis is waiting. The sun is shining brightly on this cloudless day, causing the snow to burn my eyes.

"Have fun?" Lewis taunts as I slide into the back of the car.

I blush. "He helps me to write," I admit shyly.

Lewis smiles, "what are we doing today?"

"I wanted to get more clothes from my room at The Lodge, and then I thought we could have lunch together before you drop me back."

"That sounds nice," the indicator ticking as he turns out of the trailer park.

"Did you really find your lumberjack?"

He laughs, "no, maybe tonight," but his words don't sound sincere. I try to process the meaning behind it, but decide that maybe I am reading too much into his tone.

We sit at our window spot, waiting for our lunch with a glass of wine, Lewis has a beer instead; and I was beginning to love our intimate moments together. The fact that we can comfortably sit in silence has me realising just how much I trust Lewis.

He clears his throat. "Are you sure about Atlas?"

His question catches me off guard. "What do you mean?" I ask hesitantly.

He drops his gaze from mine. "I mean...you said it was intense- and I just want to make sure you are okay?" He looks to me again.

"You said intense means passionate?"

"Yeah I did, it's just sometimes that can also mean dangerous..."

I can't quite understand where this sudden change is coming from, and I lift my knit higher up my neck. "I think he is danger-ous...just not to me."

Lewis takes a sip of his drink as the waitress places our food in front of us, leaving us awkwardly waiting for her to leave. "I just want you to know that if you need to talk to me, you can and I won't judge anything; all I care about is your safety."

I reach for his hand across the table and give it a small squeeze. "You are a true friend Lewis. Atlas is very much intense in every conceivable way, and I wouldn't-" I stop myself, not knowing how much I should divulge to Lewis. "I wouldn't say our relationship is normal, but...but I think he is the safest person I could ever be around."

He seems satisfied with my answer, giving me a small smile before digging into his food. "Okay, when do I get to meet him? And when are you bringing Bre?" Something sparks across his eyes and I hide my smile with a bite of my salad.

"Soon," I promise.

Lewis and I get a coffee and a cake after our lunch, talking more about my story and the ideas I have, which is not something I would ever do with anyone other than my mother and Bre, but Lewis is quickly becoming one of my most favourite people; almost like a family member. I grab some more of my things from my room before doing a quick grocery shop, then Lewis drops me back to Atlas's trailer, the smoke from his chimney billowing in the clear sky.

I do some tidying of his trailer before preparing a lasagne and placing it in his range. I smile as I think of Atlas coming home to his clean house with dinner cooking for him. No punishments this time, although a jolt of electricity runs through me as I think of defying him. I love the way his eyes darken when I push him, the fear that causes my heart to race as I watch all the way he contemplates torturing me. I sit on his bed with my laptop, waiting for him to come home, and as the sun sets; I know it will be soon. The excitement builds as I hear a truck pull up, feeling as giddy as a schoolgirl with her first crush.

There is a quick knock on the door before it is opened. "Atlas!" A mans voice calls out and I feel immediate fear.

Within a second, a tall man is standing in front of the table, looking directly at me with some confusion. His hair is dark blonde, but buzz cut short and his eyes are green...He must be Atlas's brother or cousin.

"Well hello," he smiles and moves to the end of the bed. His confusion long gone as a predatory smile moves across his lips. I swallow at my dry throat.

"Atlas isn't home yet," I say quietly.

"I can see that, and who are you?"

"Isobel," I attempt to say louder. His mouth and nose are different, but a lot of this man looks like Atlas.

"I'm Lars, Atlas's brother." He sits on the end of the bed and extends his hand for me to shake.

Cautiously, I place my hand in his and he rips me closer to him. I gasp out in shock, "you are quite beautiful," he whispers.

I attempt to move from his grip and hungry eyes. "I- I'm with your brother," I fight.

His smirk grows. "We have shared girls before Isobel."

My mouth pops open, and his eyes light up with my surprise. "I'm not that kind of girl," I breathe nervously.

He shrugs, standing from the bed to move away from me. He takes off his jacket, seemingly making himself at home, and my eyes dart to his arms. To the marks that cover him, and without tattoos, his are more obvious. I suck in a deep breath as I look at the evidence of his abuse, the abuse they both have endured. I cough and advert my gaze. "I'm sure he won't be much longer," I say to try and fight off the awkwardness.

"I am aware of my brother's work times," he replies sarcastically.

"Good for you," I retort, without realising that I have just bit back at him.

He looks to me again and smirks, his eyes dancing like this is some kind of game. He opens the range to look at the lasagne. "Want me to stay for dinner?"

"Not particularly," I smile politely.

He laughs, "you are going to be trouble, aren't you Izzy?"

"Isobel," I reply sternly.

And before Lars can reply, Atlas storms inside. "Ahh brother, Izzy was just inviting me to stay for dinner."

Atlas's jaw clenches at the use of the pet name Izzy. "Not tonight. What are you doing here?"

The lightness moves from Lars as he motions with his head for them to go outside. Atlas nods as Lars grabs his jacket before moving past him. "I won't be long," he smiles at me before heading outside after Lars.

The range begins beeping at me and I jump, releasing a long breath that I didn't realise I was holding.

CHAPTER NINETEEN

ISOBEL

Atlas comes back inside just as I am placing the plates on the table for us to eat. "Smells delicious," he closes the distance between us, grabbing the back of my neck and consuming me with his mouth. "I fucking missed you," he pulls away and rests his forehead against mine.

"I missed you," I whisper breathlessly.

We sit down and start eating, almost like we have done this a hundred times before. "So Lars is...interesting," I finally say.

Atlas pauses the chewing in his mouth. "What did he say to you?"

I push my food around, avoiding his darkened gaze. "That you used to um...share girls."

He smirks before slowly lifting his beer to his lips. "Only the ones I don't care about."

"And me...?"

"I will never share you with another soul Petal, you are mine."

"Why did he need to talk to you in private?"

"Just work stuff," He places another forkful in his mouth.

"Lumberjack meetings need to happen in private?" I challenge.

He smirks at this. "His work, not mine."

"And what does Lars do for work?" I lift my own drink to my mouth.

"So many questions tonight, Petal, it's almost like you are begging me to keep your mouth full." I choke on my drink, my cheeks instantly heating; and he smiles at my reaction. "Lars is an entrepreneur," he says simply, and I roll my eyes.

"Isobel, did you just roll your eyes? And here I was thinking there would be no punishments tonight."

My thighs press together as his eyes devour my face, savouring the way he makes me squirm. I don't let him distract me though, "and do you help with this entrepreneuring?"

His jaw moves slightly with amusement. "I handle the clients that don't feel like paying."

I nod my head, of course he does. Atlas is the perfect man for that job. "He- he has scars like yours," I whisper.

"He was only physically abused."

I nod my head again, the thoughts of my own invisible scars coming to the surface. I was almost expecting Mum to ring me today and tell me they found my cousin. I hate that he is missing, it has me on edge in ways I never imagined, when Atlas is home though; I know that I am safe.

"Do I need to fuck my brother from your mind, Petal?"

My head snaps up to his, "I- wasn't thinking about Lars."

"What are you thinking about?"

"It's nothing important."

He rips my chair closer to his, his mouth so close that I can feel his warm breath. "What were you thinking about Isobel?"

"It's just my cousin..." his eyes darken at the mention of him. "My mum called me to let me know that he is missing, and it just has me on edge is all. I know it's silly, he would have no way of knowing where I am, but- it still scares me, I guess."

"You don't need to be scared of anything but me Petal," he keeps me close to his body; his eyes never leaving mine.

"When you go to work is the only time I feel afraid," I whisper.

"You don't need to be afraid Isobel," he says calmly.

A slight amount of anger builds in my chest. "You can't just tell me how I should feel and then hope my emotions will follow through."

He smiles darkly, "Isobel, you have nothing to fear from your cousin."

"What, why?"

"Because," he places his hand against my cheek, his thumb lightly stroking my skin. "I killed him."

I remain still as he continues to stroke my skin and stare into my eyes, his words attempting to retain inside my brain. Eventually I giggle, I giggle until I begin laughing and Atlas starts laughing with me, leaning back, and sipping on his beer; his eyes still watching mine.

I killed him.

My laughter stops cold and my face drops, "you are being serious...?"

"I never joke about killing Petal, but it does get my dick hard seeing how funny you find it."

I automatically look down at his length straining against his jeans. My body begins shaking slightly. "W-when?" I stammer.

"When you went back to Chicago, I hunted him down, tortured him, and then killed him," he says in a way someone would talk about taking their puppy for a walk.

"What if I had more than one cousin?" I ask, shaking.

He shrugs, "I would have murdered them all just to be safe."

My jaw drops, "Atlas-"

"Yes Petal?"

I get up from my chair, needing to put a bit of distance between us. "Y-you can't just murder people!" I begin pacing. "What if someone finds out?" My pacing becomes more erratic. "This is too far; this is completely insane Atlas-"

My pacing is cut off as he slams me against a wall, knocking the breath out of me. He pins me by my throat, "I can and will do whatever the fuck I want to the people that hurt you Petal." I blink slowly before swallowing. "I murdered for you, that's how insane you make me Isobel, and you want to know something truly terrifying?"

"What?" I whisper, too scared to move an inch.

"I would kill every day for the rest of my life if it means keeping you safe."

Tears fall down my cheeks at his words. "I- I don't know if I am okay with this," I admit.

"You keep talking like I don't understand you; I see you so clearly baby, I know what you do in that head of yours when someone does wrong by you. You punish them. How many times did you punish your cousin with your mind?"

"Thousands," I breathe.

"And was it ever enough? Was it ever justice?"

I shake my head, "no."

He begins unbuttoning my jeans. "Let me be your justice baby, your punisher, your executioner."

"You killed for me," I breathe.

"Yes Petal, I killed for you, I tortured for you, I would do fucking anything for you. I own you, but can't you see that you own me? That you have all of me so consumed with you that someone looking at you for too long makes me want to murder them."

I fumble for his jeans as my mouth crashes against his, not caring about our teeth clashing, not caring about how rough he will be. "I need you Atlas, so fucking hard."

He smirks against my mouth. "Oh, I have a surprise you will truly love Petal."

Chapter Twenty

Isobel

He lifts me, kissing me as he walks me to his two-seater dark leather couch, placing me down; he turns on his TV. "What-"

"All will be answered soon baby," he goes to a drawer and pulls out a USB before shoving it into the TV, then he comes back to undress me. Pulling my jeans down and lifting my knit over my head, my heart pounds with anticipation. As he removes my bra and panties, I reach for his shirt, but he stops my greedy hands.

"That's not fair," I pout.

He smirks before sitting beside me and then pulls me onto his lap, so that my back is against his chest and we are both staring at the screen. I can feel his hardness beneath me and I squirm, hating the way his jeans are stopping our friction.

Then the screen comes to life, and my cousin is tied to a chair. Pure terror climbs its way up my throat, "Atlas-" I panic.

"Shh," he whispers, stroking my hair.

I can see my cousin's tears streaking his dirty face. *"Please,"* he calls out.

"Atlas- I don't want to watch this," the fear begins raking its way along my body.

"Petal I did this for you," his hand trails from my head down to my breasts.

Atlas steps onto the screen. Only you couldn't tell that it's him. His entire body is covered with dark clothing and his face has a skull mask concealing him, but I know him so well that it is clearly him. "Please," I whisper, "I don't think I can watch this."

"Then why are your nipples hard for me Petal?" He lightly grazes his fingers along them, torturing me slowly. "You will watch what I did for you, and you will let me know if the punishment was enough."

I turn my head to his. "It is enough Atlas; I don't need to watch this to know what you have done for me."

He roughly forces my head back to the screen. "You will watch, you will take pleasure in his suffering as I pleasure you." I suck in a deep breath as he pinches my nipple, causing my back to arch into him. "Good girl," he whispers against my ear.

"Do you know why you are here?" Atlas asks my cousin, but his voice has been changed within the mask, he has left nothing to chance.

"N-no, " my cousin stutters.

"You hurt someone that means everything to me."

"Please, I will do anything, please this is sick!"

"You are sick Micheal, and you must be punished."

Atlas brings his fingers to my lips, "spit baby," he orders.

I do what he says and spit onto his fingers, and he bites my earlobe. "You are so fucking sexy." He spreads my legs and then begins rubbing my spit around my entrance.

"I am going to make this slow Micheal, so it will be fun for the both of us," Atlas picks up a knife and moves closer to him.

I squirm against his touch as he continues to rub but not push inside me. "I am going to take this slow baby," he whispers against my ear and I moan.

And as he cuts off my cousin's finger, he pushes one of his inside me. I clutch at his thigh, watching as my cousin screams and Atlas chucks his finger away.

"Luckily, we have nine more left."

"Please stop," my cousin begs.

And all I can think of when I hear his pleas were my own to him. How I begged him to get off me, how I begged him to stop touching me, and as Atlas cuts off his second finger; I smile.

"I told you; you would like it Petal," he groans against my ear as he adds another finger. "So fucking tight," he breathes.

With all of my cousin's fingers gone, his head hangs low as he sobs in pain, the blood coating Atlas's knife; the knife he begins trailing to his face. "Where should we have fun next, Micheal?"

"Please, just let me go, I can't do this anymore," he cries.

"You know who else begged you to stop?"

"Please..."

"Say her fucking name Micheal." He shakes his head back and forth, but Atlas grabs the back of his head, driving the knife

straight into his eyeball and cutting it out. Micheal's screams are louder than any I have ever heard.

Then he adds another finger, stretching me slowly as I begin to close my legs, but he rips them back open. "My dick is bigger than three fingers, be a good girl and fucking take it Petal."

"Say her name." He moves the knife to his other eye.

"Isobel," he cries a mixture of blood and tears.

My breath catches as Atlas quickens his pace and I watch him cut my cousin's other eye out. As I get close to finishing, my head drops back against his chest, my eyes closing in pleasure. Atlas pinches my nipple so hard I cry out from the pain. "Eyes open Petal, you will cum watching or you won't cum at all."

"Please," I beg Atlas at the same time as my cousin does.

"Please what?" he whispers against my ear.

"Make me cum- I need it Atlas, I need you please."

"You sound so nice begging for me like the beautiful whore you are, a whore only for me."

"Only you," I moan out as he shoves his fingers down my throat before pushing them back inside me. My eyes watching as Atlas cuts his mouth, giving him a smiley.

"See how incredible you taste," and I moan as his other hand makes its way back to my nipple.

Then he swaps the knife for a cleaver, swinging it down and removing both of his hands, then he moves to his feet, breaking each one of his toes before butchering them off. At one point my cousin passes out from the pain, but Atlas puts something under his nose which has him screaming once more. "I'm going to cum," I moan out, digging my nails into his thighs.

"Yes baby, cum to the grand finale," his fingers curling inside me quicker.

My cousin must be close to bleeding out by now. Atlas cuts his dick off and forces him to choke on it. I cum violently on his lap as my cousin has nothing left to scream, nothing left to give but small whimpers as his eyes grow heavy and his head flops to the side.

The aftershocks of my orgasm have me twitching against Atlas's hard dick. "Well," he nips at my ear. "Was the punishment as good as the ones you gave in your mind?"

I rush off his lap, desperately trying to pull his jeans down, he helps me by lifting his hips, and once his jeans and underwear are far enough down, I jump back onto him, easing the tip of his cock into my pussy. "It was perfect," I admit, not letting my brain think too long about how sick I am, the consuming need to have him fill me far outweighs that. He grabs my hips as I slowly move down his length, sinking my teeth into my bottom lip. "This is too deep..." I have him all the way inside me, but I can't move without the size of him feeling like it is ripping me apart.

"Petal if you don't start fucking me, I will slam you down onto my cock so hard your organs will be rearranged."

I open my scrunched eyes to look into his deadly serious ones before I begin to slowly move up and down him. He groans, digging his fingers into my ass so hard I know I will have fresh bruises tomorrow. The thought exhilarates me. Having Atlas mark me how he wants causes me to fuck him faster.

"Fuck Petal," his head falls back to the couch and I grab him by the mouth to look back at me.

"Eyes on me baby," I smirk as his shocked eyes grow big.

He places his arms behind his head with a smug grin. "Want to talk big? Fuck me until I fill you up Petal."

I kiss him, moving my hips faster until the pressure is too much that my orgasm flows out of me. My pace slowing and jolting with the shocks, so he grabs my ass and fucks me so hard and fast that I scream loudly.

"Everyone in this park is going to hear what my dick does to you Petal, now beg for it."

"Please cum inside me!"

He groans loudly before spilling himself into me, thrusting a couple more times before my forehead rests against his.

"Oh god," I whisper.

"God turned away from you the moment you came on my fingers to dismemberment. I am the devil baby, now show me who you worship, I want to see you taste both of us."

Chapter Twenty-one

Atlas

Obsession is no longer the right fucking word for what I feel for my Petal. There is no word in any language to describe what I feel, because what we have is non-existent. We created something new and so fucking beautiful I almost can't stand it. I cannot stand that there will never be enough, the wanting only grows every time I watch her.

Like now, she is sleeping on her stomach so peacefully, my shirt has bunched up so that her perfect ass is out. I can see the small bruises forming from my fingers and I grow hard as I realise her pussy is glistening from my cum. I am about to undress and push back inside her when my brain forces me to stop.

You have a job to do.

It causes me physical pain to walk away from her, but I can't have her awake right now, and no matter how slow I fuck her; she will wake up as I stretch her perfect cunt with my dick.

I quietly open the wood heater to place another log in, I chuck the USB of me torturing her cousin in at the same time. The only evidence left of his murder. Part of me thought I would be holding onto it for much longer. Once I saw the worry cross her face and the fear she was feeling when I leave, I couldn't not tell her. She needs to know that no one will be left unpunished for hurting her. I have tried to find the three men that nearly raped her outside of The Pike, but they fled that night, and no one has heard from them since. Smart men, but I will find them, and I will follow through this time. My nightmares are filled with them pinning her down as she stares at them with an empty soul. I should have killed them when I had the chance, fuck what Isobel thought. We are so destined to one another that I could have still made her mine after murder. Nothing would have stopped us, and now those three men get to plague my sleep like the fucking vermin they are. I hope they spend every second in agonising fear, just knowing that I am coming for them.

The thought gets me hard again, murdering them slowly and then fucking Petal with their blood still splattered across my body. Jesus, I need to stop my thoughts of her or I will never get anything done. I softly tuck the sheet up higher on her body before grabbing my pack and leaving.

Lewis is not outside tonight, I guess he took my advice seriously; although we exchanged numbers and I told him he could call me if he needed.

I head to the first address Lars sent to me, there is a light snow flittering around my headlights as I drive down the empty road. Devils Lake isn't busy at this time of night on a weekday, luckily I don't have work tomorrow; or I would be getting no sleep at all. The thought that I get to spend a whole day with Isobel is fucking intoxicating. I turn off the headlights before turning into the first driveway. Shutting off my truck, I reach for my bag, checking the clip of my M17 pistol before reaching for my skull mask. When I first started doing this for Lars, I had an asshole hold his phone up and tell me he was live filming. He wasn't, but it was incentive enough to start hiding my identity. Everyone knows who I am, but with the mask, there is no way to prove it. The soft snow lightly falls on me as I check for an unlocked door or window.

I find a window around the side of his trashed house unlocked. I quietly slide it open before stealthing my way through his home. It fucking stinks like mouldy socks, beer and weed. I find him asleep in his underwear on a worn-down couch. There is a naked girl asleep tucked in his arm. I sigh. Why do drug addicts have to live so feral? I stand over him, he can't be much older than me, but I think the drugs are beginning to age him. I slowly slide the barrel of my gun into his open mouth. He stirs immediately, attempting to move what is bothering him from his face, only to smack my gun and wake with a jolt.

Once he realises who is standing over him, and what is rammed down his throat, his eyes grow large with panic and he starts shaking his head. His muffled no's around my gun wake his crack whore. She takes one look at me and begins screaming. I raise my finger to my lips, telling her to be quiet. She does, but she begins sobbing as she covers her breasts with her arms.

"You're late," I say calmly.

I remove my gun to let him spout out whatever bullshit fucking excuse he has. He raises his hands and sits up. "I know- look, I am so sorry; I can get the money."

"I know you will get the money," I smile even though he can't see it. I place my gun in the back of my pants and watch as relief flickers across his eyes. Just as quickly as I put my gun away, I snap his arm in one movement that has the whore screaming again, and him groaning as he clenches his arm to his chest. "You have one week, or next time it will be your fucking neck."

I leave out the front door to the sounds of that bitch crying. I have yet to follow through with a death threat for my brother, they always seem to find the money; some broken bones just help kick them into gear.

Then I drive back to the park, the next client is a neighbour of mine, one I have visited regularly. I pull up at my trailer before walking around the snow filled paths that would usually be dirt every other time of the year; before getting to his. His porch light is always on, and I know that his door won't be locked. I tap the snow off my boots before heading inside. His trailer is far too cold for my liking, but addicts don't feel much of anything besides the high they constantly chase. He is asleep is his room, and I kick his foot that is hanging off his bed.

He awakes immediately, his eyes blinking a couple times to register his surroundings. I never wear my mask with this man. "Hi Atlas," his dry voice croaks out.

"Jerry."

"I thought I'd be seeing you soon," he begins sitting up.

"You are starting to look a little like death, Jerry. Think it's time you cut back?"

He nods his head, "working on it."

"You know why I am here."

"Could we just do a finger this time? I think I am getting too old for arms and legs."

I sigh, "how about we make a deal?" I hated hurting this man.

"What kind?"

"You cut back, give the money to Lars in two days, and I won't break anything tonight."

"You'd do that for me?"

I begin walking out of his tiny room. "Two days Jerry, otherwise I am coming back and breaking both arms."

"Thank you!" He calls as I walk out the front door.

I am desperate to get back to my little Petal, tucked perfectly amongst my sheets.

CHAPTER TWENTY-TWO

Isobel

I wake to the door shutting loudly. I sit up in bed, clutching Atlas's sheets to my chest. I blink several times as my eyes adjust to the flames that push light towards me. Then I see him, head to toe in black, with his skull mask on. My heart thunders in my chest as the grogginess of sleep fades away.

"Where have you been?" I ask, my voice raspy from sleep.

He removes his gloves and slowly walks towards me, a hunter moving in on his prey. I swallow away my fear. The fear of it not actually being him, although I know it is. I know his build and muscles like a painting I have spent my whole life gazing at.

I move to the end of the bed, like a moth to Atlas's constant flame; I will always be drawn to him. No traps are needed, I will glide happily to his slaughter.

I am his willing prey.

His hand lightly strokes my cheek, and I flinch at the coldness; the small specs of snow are beginning to dissolve into his darkness. Where I know I will soon dissolve too. His thumb presses against my bottom lip, parting my mouth slightly as I gaze up at his mask, at the green eyes that spark his fire. Even with the mask, I can tell the need he has for me from his darkened gaze. Ever so slowly, he slides his thumb past my lips and into my warm mouth, I swipe my tongue along his cold skin before slowly sucking.

He can't help but let out a small groan, and I press my thighs together to stop the ache spreading through my core. The ache that only he can fill. He unbuttons his belt with one hand, removing his thumb from my mouth, he slowly slides himself in; stopping when I let out a slight choke. I look up to him as he fucks my mouth painfully slow, his grip on the back of my neck causes me to moan around him. He lets out another groan as I begin so suck him faster and harder, wanting my throat sore, wanting the memory of him fucking my mouth so hard; I feel it for days.

I imagine him smirking behind the mask at my desperation for him. He wraps my hair around his hand to stop me from sucking him too fast, wanting me to beg for him to fuck my throat raw. I decide to play along with his game, a game I know he will win regardless; lightly I use my teeth along him and he stills completely. Ripping his cock from my mouth, he roughly squeezes my cheeks together, but I want to push him further; so I smile up at him.

Taunting him, even though he has all the control. His mask tilts to the side as he contemplates what to do with me, and my heart speeds up as I watch all the ways he wants to punish me. He keeps his hand squeezing my face as he reaches behind himself, then he strokes a gun against my head. "Want to play Petal?"

My breath hitches as he drops my face, letting the gun lightly caress down my cheek as I work to control my panicked breaths. "Atlas..." I warn.

"Come now Petal, you were willing to play Russian Roulette with your teeth and my cock."

The gun slowly drops from my face, moving down my chest. "I'm sorry," I whisper.

"Your smile before said otherwise, you wanted me to punish you." He lifts the mask and I see his darkened smirk, the smirk I know that won't be satisfied with apologies now.

I reach for his hard dick again, hoping to distract him. "Please fuck my mouth Atlas."

He chuckles, "I do love your begging baby, but only good girls go unpunished. Are you a good girl Isobel?"

"Yes," I whisper as he spreads my legs with the barrel of his gun.

He shakes his head. "Lies now too?" He brings the gun to his mouth, spits on the barrel, before rubbing it around to lubricate the weapon.

"Atlas- please, I am sorry." There isn't much I know about guns, but I do not know that they should not go inside me.

He pins my legs apart as the tip of the gun presses against my opening. He rubs it around; the coldness causing me to flinch. I watch as he leans his head in between my legs and spits more onto my pussy. I squirm as the gun continues to tease my entrance. Slowly he begins to push it inside, I grab the sheets as the unfamiliar hardness fills me. I wince at the discomfort, but once the gun is all the way inside, Atlas groans loudly.

"Now you are a good girl Petal, look how well your pussy swallows my gun." I try to watch, but as he slowly begins to fuck me with the barrel, my head flops back down. The discomfort replaced with pleasure as I attempt to stop the moans leaving my mouth. Not wanting to give him the satisfaction that I am actually enjoying this.

"You can't hide from me Petal; I know you are enjoying have a loaded weapon fuck your perfect cunt." I moan loudly as he fucks me faster. "Cum over my gun baby." My body tightens and then explodes. Before I have time to process my orgasm, he removes the gun and shoves it into my mouth. "Clean it." I do what he asks, sucking myself from his gun. Knowing in this moment, there isn't anything I would deny this man. He tosses the gun to the side, shoving his dick back down my throat, and fucking me so hard; I have to work to keep my eyes on him. "This what you wanted?"

I moan my approval as he relentlessly fucks my mouth. "Such a good girl," he holds my head in place as he thrusts in and out. He groans loudly as the warmth of his cum shoots to the back of my throat. I swallow him down greedily as the last of his spurts jolt free. He breathes heavily as he looks down at me, and as he removes himself from my mouth, his thumb is back to lightly caress my lips.

"Fucking perfect," he whispers.

CHAPTER TWENTY-THREE

ISOBEL

"Where were you?" The sun is beginning to rise as I lay cuddled against Atlas's chest.

"Entrepreneuring," his fingers lightly graze my arm.

"I don't like it. What if you get hurt?"

"Nothing can hurt me but you, Petal."

"I'm serious Atlas, what if something happened to you?" The thought of him being hurt makes me feel murderous.

"Isobel, that is something you never need to worry about. I was taught a great number of ways on how to kill a man, including thirty ways with just my bare hands."

I suck in a deep breath, exhaustion beginning to settle behind my eyes. "Do you ever have PTSD from when you served?"

"No baby, killing doesn't really affect me."

"Do you ever miss it?" I yawn, stretching my arms out.

"I miss my brothers," he admits.

"Why did you stop?"

"Mum died, and Lars needed me." I never thought to ask about where his mother was now.

"How long ago did she die?"

"Three years. That night you came up to me at the bar was her anniversary." I remember his dead eyes looking into mine as he told me to fuck off.

"I'm sorry," I whisper.

"She was a crack whore, but there were some nice memories early on." I squeeze my body against him tighter. "You are my home now Isobel," he kisses my head as sleep calmly claims me.

I wake just after ten in the morning, Atlas is still fast asleep beside me. I quietly climb out of bed to go to the bathroom, not wanting to wake him. Sometimes it feels like he never sleeps, and I know he doesn't get enough of it. I sit in his warm shower, remembering the things Atlas did to me the night before. He murdered my cousin and made me orgasm to his torture. I didn't really know what I believed in, but if there is a hell; I am surely walking through those gates now.

He murdered for me, he would do it again, he would punish me in ways I never imagined; and I couldn't walk away even if I wanted. He would find me, and maybe I would always find him too. We are most definitely sick, last night proved that, but maybe it also proved that there is no one else for us.

So our love is sick, and I am okay with that. Maybe I am destined for hell, and if I am; Atlas would be coming with me. I pity the devil for when he has to meet him, because Atlas would turn wherever we are into his kingdom; and murder anyone that even looked at me.

As I dry myself, I smile at the new bruises that have his finger indents. The way Atlas fucks me is like he is trying to morph our bodies as one. I decide to cook us bacon and eggs, he manages to stay asleep while I cook. Just as I am dishing up, I hear his phone vibrate. Ignoring it, I continue to load up our plates, but the phone vibrates again. It's not like he hasn't been through my phone, I shrug as I pick it up. He has no password, and I can see it's Lars messaging him, asking him to come to his tonight because he is having a party.

"Find anything interesting?"

I jump, dropping his phone to the ground. "Sorry!" I reach to pick it up.

"Becoming just as obsessive as me Petal?"

I roll my eyes and hand him his phone. "Lars wants you to go to his tonight."

"Pass. What smells amazing?"

He hops out of bed naked, my eyes immediately soaking all of him up as he puts on a pair of briefs. "I made some eggs, why don't you want to go?"

"Because I want to be with you," he kisses me softly, reaching around to grab both of our plates and take them to his table.

I follow him with our cutlery. "Well, why don't we go together?"

He pauses, watching me. "It won't be fun."

I shrug, moving around the scrambled eggs on my plate. "I wouldn't mind meeting the people you are friends with."

"I don't really have friends, just Lars."

"I think it would be fun, I could get to know your brother more, and we can have a few drinks together."

"If you really want to go, we can," he places some bacon into his mouth.

I smile, "we can bring Lewis and you can meet him!"

"I've already met him, but sure."

"What when?"

"Not important, he can come, but the second you want to leave, we are leaving."

"Okay," I place a forkful of eggs in my mouth, my throat hurting as I swallow.

"What are you thinking about Petal?"

"Nothing."

"Your cheeks have gone the delicious pink shade they go when I fuck you."

"My throat is just a little sore," my cheeks heat further as I picture how hard he fucked my mouth.

"Good," he smirks.

"I was wondering how you would feel about meeting my best friend?" I ask before he takes me on this table.

"Bre?"

"Do you just know everything about me?"

"She is the only other person you ring or message besides Lewis and your mum."

I raise my eyebrows at him.

"Surely you aren't about to judge me for something I just caught you doing?"

My cheeks heat once more, "is that a yes?"

"If she is important to you, then yes baby."

"She is more than important; she is like my sister."

"Then she is my family also."

CHAPTER TWENTY-FOUR

ATLAS

I really don't fucking want to go to my brothers, but Isobel is all excited about it now. Singing as she applies her makeup in my bathroom. I want to keep her locked up for myself, not letting any other man's gaze cross her. Plus, I know some of the low lives that will be attending tonight, and now I'm going to have to murder people.

I stoke the fire and see Lewis's headlights pull in. "Lewis is here."

"Okay, nearly ready!" She rushes out in a tiny skirt with tights, a warm knit and knee-high boots. I am definitely fucking murdering someone tonight.

"Petal..."

"Atlas?"

"Do you want people to die tonight?"

She looks at me confused. "Why would people need to die?"

"Can't you wear anything but that?"

"Anything?" She teases.

I sigh, "fine, their blood is on your hands."

"You are being dramatic," she smiles.

I pull her close to me. "No Petal, being dramatic would be me tying you to my bed and never letting you leave."

Her eyes dance with that need to push me, and my dick twitches in response. I'm starting to think that my little Petal enjoys being punished. She presses her lips against mine. "Lewis is here," she reminds me sweetly before turning away from me, heading for the door.

It is a still night, without a spec of snow falling or a breeze to push the coldness around our bodies. Isobel slides into the car first, excitedly saying hello to Lewis. "Lewis," I greet.

"Atlas," he smiles back.

"Lewis, could you please enlighten me on how the two of you have met?" She asks him.

I place my hand high on Isobel's thigh as she clips in her seatbelt. "Small town and all," Lewis waves his hand to dismiss the question. I'm starting to like this guy even more. I wasn't entirely sure how she would react to me basically egging Lewis on to fight me. "Do you really want me to come with you? I don't mind just dropping you both off."

"Of course I want you to come, plus you never know who you might meet," Isobel says suggestively.

"I guess it will be nice to get out of The Lodge for a bit."

I give Lewis the address of Lars's house and as he begins driving out of the trailer park; I move my hand further up Isobel's thigh. She rips her head to me, her eyes wide. I lean in close, pressing my lips against her ear. "You wanted to wear the skirt Petal," my hand begins rubbing slowly.

"With tights," she whispers back, biting her bottom lip.

I rip her tights just enough for my hand to slip in. She attempts to hide her gasp and I hide my groan at feeling her silk thong. I fucking love her different lacy and silk numbers she wears. I remove my hand only to quietly spit on my fingers, then I move her thong to the side as I slide two fingers straight in.

She squeezes my thigh hard as her head flops back against the seat. "Will there be many people there tonight?" Lewis asks.

"Maybe fifty," I respond as Isobel lets out a tiny moan. "Quiet baby," I whisper in her ear, plunging my fingers as deep as they can go. My perfect Petal spreads her legs wider for me, always so slutty for my touch. God, I want to fuck her so fucking bad. At this point I couldn't care less if Lewis sees. But I can't murder someone Isobel cares about, and if he saw the way her face looks while getting fucked- I'd have no other choice.

"Do you want to stop and get drinks?" Lewis turns a corner and we are getting close to our destination.

"No, there will be plenty where we are going." Isobel sinks her teeth into my neck to stifle her moans. Her hand moves to my painfully hard dick, rubbing me hard as my fingers bring her close to the edge that only I can take her to. She has a sharp intake of breath as her teeth bite harder into my skin, and then I feel her body jolting against my fingers. Her teeth leave my neck, but her pants remain against my skin as I slowly remove my fingers; only to shove them into her mouth. She sucks my fingers like she is starving and I can't help but groan as I watch her.

"Is this the place?"

Lewis turns into Lars's driveway. "Yeah it is." Isobel read-justs her skirt as she takes in the driveway lined with different trucks and cars. There is a low thump from the music, and flames from a fire outside. "Not too late to go home."

"It will be nice," she persists.

"I highly doubt that," I reply, grabbing her hand.

"It may surprise you," Lewis says before getting out.

"I am going to take you into a room and fuck you so hard, you will wish you never came here Petal," I say against her mouth before getting out. She follows after me, her cheeks a perfect shade of pink.

The three of us walk together, Isobel's hand tight in mine; I can see Lars laughing by the large fire. A beer in his hand, as he moves to whisper something in a girl's ear. "Atlas!" He lifts both hands in the air to greet us. "Izzy," he smiles playfully, and the urge to smash my hand in his throat is high.

"Hello Lars," she says politely.

"And who is this?" Lars extends his hand to Lewis.

"Lewis," he takes his hand with a smile.

"I didn't think you would actually come brother, now that Izzy has you cooped up all the time." His eyes briefly dart to my neck; to the bite wound that I know is forming.

"Isobel is the reason we are here."

She smiles in a smart-ass way to Lars, and now I want to fuck her even more. "Well, come enjoy yourselves," he extends his arm for us to keep walking.

A few people greet me as we walk past the fire to the front porch that is all open. People are sitting on lounges smoking weed, and there is a tattoo machine that is also being used on a guy. The music is louder inside the house, and just before we can enter, a girl stops Lewis to talk to him. Isobel waits for him, but he gives her a nod that says they will catch up later. "Come with me," I grip her hand tighter as I move to the back of the house. I hear a girl call out to me, but I ignore her. There is only one thing fucking blinding my mind right now. I need to bury myself so deep inside Petal that she screams louder than this music.

I open a door, taking us into a plain room with a double bed. Shutting the door helps to drown out the music slightly. "Whose room is this?" She walks around looking for anything significant.

"Mine, when I stay here on occasion. Lars knows not to let anyone come in here."

"Why do you stay here on occasion?" Her hand glides along the made sheets.

"When Lars needs help with things."

She scoffs. "Is this where you shared girls?"

"Do you really want the answer to that?" I head for my wooden cupboard, opening the first drawer to a gun, some knives and rope. I pull the rope out and turn back to Isobel.

"I guess not," she admits as she flops onto the bed. Her eyes grow wide when she takes in the rope I'm holding. "What are you doing?" She whispers.

"Did you think my threat in the car was empty, Petal?"

"No," she whispers nervously.

"Then be a good girl and undress for me."

She starts with her boots, and then stands to remove the rest of her clothing, my dick instantly getting hard as I take in her breathtaking body. A body that is all mine to do with as I please. Isobel has proved time and time again that she can't deny me and my needs. She would let me ruin every inch of her if I wanted.

And fuck did I want to.

I move to gently caress her face before I tie her hands firmly in front of her. "Lay on your stomach, Isobel."

Her eyes stare into mine, and I wonder for a moment if she will defy me. If she will push me the way I know she loves to do. She breaks my stare first and does what she is told. I can't help the smirk that pulls at my mouth.

I tie the remaining rope to the bedhead, making sure there is no way she can escape. "You won't hurt me, will you?" Her breathing hitches with fear and my dick strains harder against my jeans.

"And how would you plan on stopping me, Petal? Your whole body is mine for the taking, for as long as I like. I plan on worshiping it in a way I deem worthy." I lightly trace my fingers down her back. "But if I do hurt you, just know you won't be alone in that pain baby; that is always a pledge."

I watch as the goosebumps rise across her back from my touch. "Atlas..."

"Tell me you would deny me nothing Petal, tell me you would let me do every sick fantasy I want to you."

She is already a little breathless and we haven't even begun. "My body is yours to do with as you please."

"Such a good fucking girl for me."

CHAPTER TWENTY-FIVE

ISOBEL

Atlas ties a shirt around my head to blindfold me, and with my sight gone; the fear etches further into my skin. "I will be back in a sec," he smacks my butt before I hear the door open and shut. Terror encompasses me as I attempt to move my hands from the rope. Why would he leave me like this? I swallow at the panic rising in my throat as I hear the door open and shut once more.

"Atlas?" I breathe.

"Yeah baby?"

"Please don't ever leave me like this again," the fear begins to dissipate.

"Oh Petal, I would never let anyone but me see you this way, they would be dead before they could even try to leave the room. Fucking hell, the sight of you right now is heaven." I feel the bed sag down from his weight as I attempt to control the flutters building in my chest.

"Well, you took my sight."

"Is that attitude, Petal? Would you like me to fix it for you?"

I remain quiet because the last time I pushed Atlas; I ended up with a gun inside me. I feel the warmth from him over me, before his lips gently kiss the top of my back. Slowly making his way down, he spreads my legs wider as he kisses the top of my ass cheek. He groans as he spreads my pussy with his fingers, his tongue pushing deep inside me; and I strain on the rope out of pleasure. Arching my hips into his face as his fingers join his tongue, he slides his tongue up to my ass and feasts on me like he is starving. "I could die right now Petal," his breath a tease buried between my legs. "I could die and be so content if this is my last meal." I moan loudly, desperately needing him to fill me.

He pulls away from me, and I feel lost without his touch. "Please," I beg.

"Yes Petal, beg for me, beg for me to fill you until you scream louder than the music."

"Please Atlas," I attempt to get on my knees, but he shoves me back down.

"I'm not done playing with you Petal," I hear a clip noise and then the sounds of him squeezing something. I lick at my lips, exhilarated and terrified for what is to come.

"I'm going to put a sniper bullet in your ass baby, it won't be thicker than my dick; but it will be deeper than my fingers." I begin to stir again, not having enough time to process how I feel about this. "Are you going to be my good girl?"

I stop my movements, wanting more than anything to please him, to satisfy every craving he has, as my thank you for bringing me back to life, as my devotion to him for bringing me feelings once more. He kisses my shoulder blade. "So perfect," he whispers.

This time he uses his fingers to spread my ass, and I feel the slippery hardness from the tip of the bullet against the tip of me. I suck in a deep breath as he slowly starts to push it inside me. I strain on the rope from the pain, and he stops to shove two fingers back inside me, fingering me slowly as he continues to push the bullet further. "Oh fuck baby, I'm going to cum over the sight of this." All of the sudden, the pain has faded as an immense pleasure takes over. He groans, "It's all the way in baby."

"Atlas?" I breathe.

"Yes Isobel?"

"It feels really fucking good," I admit.

"Do you know what good girls get?" His tone is smiling.

"Rewards?"

I feel his mouth against my ear. "They get to cum as many times as they want baby," he nips at my ear before sliding his fingers back into me, the lube from the bullet, and his spit making it so slippery. He fingers me without faltering until I cum with his name leaving my lips. I pant breathless, needing more than just his fingers inside me. "Well?" He asks.

"Again," I breathe and he chuckles.

"Such a greedy girl," but he obliges; fingering me until my body twitches, my pussy clenching his fingers, and my ass clenches around the bullet. "I could watch this all day." He gives me one more orgasm before removing his fingers, there is some movement before I hear a buzzing noise.

"W-hat is that?" The orgasms were like a drug, and now I feel like I am in a trance.

"A tattoo machine."

My eyes burst open, only to be greeted by dark fabric, the high completely wearing off as I thrash around on the bed. "What do you mean?" I ask in panic. He cannot be serious, he- he can't be. I don't have a single tattoo on me.

"Petal, you can either take this tattoo like a good girl, or you can take it like a bad one. But if you take it like a bad one, you will still be tattooed and I will punish you."

I stop my movements, "Atlas- this is too much," I whisper.

"Nothing is too much when it comes to you and me," and then he presses his hand on my lower back. "Stay still now baby." I work to control my breathing as I feel the needle press into my skin, stinging as it moves. It feels like the vibrations from the tattoo gun are vibrating the bullet, and I feel a small amount of pleasure throughout the stinging. It doesn't take long before he is done. The machine stops, Atlas slaps the small tattoo before he positions his body over mine, the tip of his dick pressing against me. "I am so fucking proud of you Petal," he rubs his dick against me, and I begin to match my hips with his rhythm; desperate to have him inside me.

"Please," I beg. With my plea, he pushes inside me, groaning as he fills me. "This is deep," I moan.

"Fuck, I can feel the bullet pushing down on my dick," he moans before kissing my back. "You feel fucking incredible baby." He begins fucking me harder. The feel of the bullet and his dick is too much, the pleasure is so overwhelming that my screams soon grow.

"Atlas," I cry out as the orgasm shocks my body.

"You don't care if you are heard do you Petal?"

"No," I moan louder, the tears stinging the edges of my eyes from all the orgasms.

"You're happy as long as your greedy holes are filled by me."

"Y-yes, - oh fuck, I'm cum-" I scream out, not knowing how many more of these I can take.

"Only. Ever. Me."

"Only you Atlas," I pant, and his grip on my ass tightens as he groans loudly, spilling himself inside me. His weight drops down and he pants on top of me as I breathe heavily into the pillow. He slowly lifts himself from me, I wince as his dick pulls out as he moves.

"You are bleeding Petal."

"Hmm?" I feel groggy as he bends down and licks the spot he tattooed.

"Mmm," he moans. "Even your fucking blood is delicious baby." Very slowly, he begins to remove the bullet, it hurts again, the way it did going in and my body tenses. "You did so well baby," he soothes, and when it is all the way out, relief fills me. Then he removes the shirt from my eyes and unties the rope with ease. I sit up, rubbing my sore wrists, and he encompasses me in his arms.

"I need to see it," I push out of his grip and move to a mirror on top of the shelves. At the very lower part of my back, just above my right ass cheek, is his name in capital letters, only about an inch thick. I- I don't even know how to think. He is permanently on me- forever. I turn around to him sitting up against the bedhead, smirking at me. "You know what this means?" I whisper.

"What Petal?"

I walk back over to the bed and straddle his lap. "It means we are forever Atlas."

He places his hands on either side of my face. "Of course Petal, there is no end for us. If you run, I will follow. If you are taken from me; I will kill everyone in this world until it is just you and I left. And when we leave this world, it will be together. It won't even end there baby, because I will find you wherever we go. If there is an afterlife, if we are ghosts wandering, if we are destined for hell, or if we are reincarnated; I will find you. Through lives, through worlds, in every fucking universe, you are mine."

I cry from his words and rest my forehead against his. "And you are mine," I whisper. "Until the darkness encompasses us."

"Oh Petal, no darkness will keep you from me. Death himself should fear me if he tried."

CHAPTER TWENTY-SIX

ISOBEL

I kiss him softly as my tears fall down my cheeks, he then begins kissing them away. "Even your tears Petal, all of you tastes like a meal I have been starved my whole life from." I feel him reaching down on the bed for something, and turn my gaze to watch what he is doing. He is pulling the tattoo machine closer to us.

I sniff, "what are you doing?"

"It's your turn now baby, our pain is united."

"I- I don't know how to do it."

"Just make sure you push the needle in deep," he switches on the machine before handing me the gun. It vibrates in my hand, and I swallow down my fear.

"Where?" I ask nervously.

He tilts his head to the side, exposing the right side of his neck to me. I rest my hand on his throat as I bring the gun to his neck. Just like signing a book Isobel, you have written your name millions of times. This is just a tad more permanent. I push the needle into his skin and flinch for him. "Deeper Petal," he encourages. I push the needle deeper into his skin and watch as a line of black ink forms the first letter. I decide to do it in cursive with a capitol I, but the rest are lower case. When I am done, there is a small amount of blood leaking from the ink, so I lean forward and lick up his neck, just like he did for mine.

"How does it look baby?"

I press my lips against his. "Like everyone will know you are mine," I say against his mouth, and he smiles into my lips.

"Now you are getting it Petal," he deepens our kiss, and I rock my hips against his hard dick. There is a loud knock at the door that causes me to jump. "Hang on!" Atlas calls out. He helps me to get dressed before stepping into his underwear and pulling up his jeans. Lars walks in before Atlas can put on his shirt.

"There you two are!" He has a beer in his hand as his eyes dart between the two of us. I can't help the warmth that moves up my neck. "If all you were going to do is fuck, why not just stay home?"

"What do you want?" Atlas says, sliding his shirt over his head.

"Can I talk to you alone?"

I roll my eyes and walk past Lars. "I'm not a snitch, you know."

He smiles down at me, "maybe not, but you are trouble Izzy."

"Careful," Atlas says darkly.

I laugh before shutting the door behind me. I should probably go check on Lewis anyway. I find him with a girl in his lap, laughing like he is the funniest man here tonight. Well that didn't take long for him. I guess he is very attractive with his short brown hair and pale blue eyes. When he drops the formal posture and relaxes, he comes across as confident; something that appeals to a lot of women. Before I can make it over to him, my path is interrupted by red hair and crooked teeth. "What are you doing here?"

Jessie has her two friends on either side of her. "Same as you," I reply sarcastically.

"Did you bring us more stuff? How thoughtful of you rich girl."

This time, I would definitely go down swinging. I'm sure Lewis will be here to drag one of them off before it gets too messy. "I'm sure she has a phone on her," the squished face says.

"I'm sure you are right Lin," Jessie says.

"Why don't you try to take it?" I smile sweetly.

"Feeling like a fight, rich girl?"

"You talk too much," I say before pulling my fist back and smashing it against her mouth. The other two jump at me, I push one away but the other drags me down, ripping at my hair as I try to fight out of her grip.

"Hey!" I hear Lewis yell, and before Lin can hit me, she is being ripped away from me. I look up to Atlas, he lifts me quickly to my feet; checking my face for any marks.

"Atlas," Jessie says nervously, the blood is spilling from her mouth, and the other two stand nervously beside her.

"What the fuck is going on?" He directs his question to the three girls.

"W-we didn't know she was with you," Jessie says.

"And you thought three against one would be courageous?" Lewis has also come to stand beside me. "What is this about Petal?"

"They stole my bag and watch on one of my first nights, and they were attempting to steal my phone tonight." I can't help but smile at the terror etched on their stupid faces.

Atlas's jaw clenches. "Get her stuff and bring it to her tonight," he says firmly. With that tone, you know there is no chance for disagreement.

"We already sold it," Jessie whispers, her gaze on her own shoes.

"How much was it worth Isobel?"

"Four thousand," I smile up at him as his hand tightens around my waist.

"You have three days to give the money back," Atlas says coldly to them.

"We didn't even get that for it-" Jessie begins to protest, but Atlas steps closer to her.

"You have three days to pay back the four grand or I will burn your fucking house to the ground. Now get the fuck out of my brother's house."

The three of them practically trip over each other to leave. "Are you okay? Why didn't you tell me?" Lewis asks.

I wave my hand, "they didn't hurt me the first night and I have plenty more bags and watches."

"Still, you should have told me," I smile at him reassuringly and hope he never finds out about the attempted sexual assault. The girl Lewis was with comes over and wraps her arms around his neck.

"I'm bored," she says to him, to which he smiles and hurries off with her.

"I see you landed the first punch," Atlas's tone is smiling, and I turn my attention back to him.

"And quite the punch she has," a girl with dark skin and chocolate eyes says. She extends her hand for me to take, and I shake hers, taking in her long braids that start from her scalp and wander far past her shoulders.

"Isobel this is Tish, the only person I would really call a friend."

"Such kind words Atlas," she smiles sarcastically.

"It's nice to meet you," I smile genuinely.

"How did Atlas manage to land you?"

I debate my answer, but decide on the truth. "He told me to fuck off, and I found that rather intriguing."

Tish bursts out into laughter, and Atlas has a smirk pulling at his mouth; a smirk that told me I would be hearing more of this later. "That sounds like Atlas, moody he is," she links her arm into mine before directing us to a free couch.

Lars also comes to sit with us, with a girl hanging from his arm, and after a few drinks and getting to know each other; I definitely enjoy Tish's company. Lars and I spend our time arguing, I realise now that he enjoys pushing my buttons, and I enjoy proving him wrong. Lewis comes back to join us and I smile at how easy and relaxed he looks. If only Bre could see him now, well she would be seeing him very soon. Maybe Devils Lake is good for Lewis, getting him out of the city.

"So what brought you to this town?" Tish asks, bringing me away from my thoughts. Lewis's eyes soften at this question, and I reach for my phone.

"I'm actually looking for this man," I hand her the phone.

"I'm sorry, I've never seen him."

Lars clicks for the phone to be passed to him, and Tish obliges. He squints at the picture. "I remember seeing him," he scratches the top of his head and I nearly jump out of the couch.

"You do!?"

He sips on his beer, "like a long time ago now, but I remember seeing him at The Pike. Who is he to you?"

"He's my father- did you see who he was with, or where he went after?" I try not to let my hopes jump too high, but Atlas's calm hand on my thigh told me I am getting too excited.

Lars shakes his head. "I left before him, and I don't think he was with anyone. I can just remember him sitting at the bar, completely shitfaced." Although my heart sinks a little, this is the first time that my father has actually been confirmed by someone that they saw him, that he was actually here.

"He's been missing for a long time now," I whisper.

"I am really sorry to hear that," Tish says, and Lars has the good sense to remain quiet for once.

"Thank you," I place my hand in Atlas's lap, the reason I have stayed in this town. The reason I can't leave.

CHAPTER TWENTY-SEVEN

ATLAS

I end up driving us home, because Lewis had far too much to drink, and we decide to stay at The Lodge tonight. Isobel unlocks the door to a cold room, with her bedside table lamp on. She flops on the bed, immediately reaching to undo her boots. "I'm going to miss your home."

"The Lodge is nice," I remove my shirt and start undoing my belt buckle.

"Yeah, but yours is homey."

"So how did you punish them?"

"Hmm?" She looks at me with those tired eyes I love so fucking much.

"When they stole your bag, what was the punishment?"

She smiles at this. "A car crash," she says simply. Like she isn't just as psychotic as me.

"I can make that happen baby," I turn to light the wood heater that the staff had already set it all for her. I turn back around to Isobel in a lacey light purple bra and matching underwear.

"I'm sure after you threatened to burn their house down, that they will find a way to get the money."

"I need to fuck you right now," my dick is hurting just looking at how the purple compliments her darker skin.

Her skin turns pink as her eyes fall to my hard dick straining against my briefs. "Why?" She whispers.

"Because I can't stand how fucking beautiful you are." I remove my briefs and stand between her legs. Her mouth parts as she continues to stare at my hard dick. "There's no time for that Petal," I spit on my hand before rubbing it onto my cock. Then I pull her purple panties to the side and slide into her. Her perfectly tight pussy hugging my cock with each thrust further in. "I'm so desperate for your cunt," she moans at my filthy mouth. Moans because no matter how much she tries to hide from all the things I want to do to her, she loves them just as much.

I flip her over, sitting on the edge of the bed while she straddles me. "I need you deeper baby," I whisper against her open mouth. She moans as she moves up and down me, her body pressed against mine is fucking ecstasy.

"Deeper," I groan, flipping her back over; I rip away her panties. Her breath hitching with the ease of it, then I place her legs on my shoulders as I push back into her. Her head flops back against the bed and she places her hands on my stomach, stopping me from going all the way inside.

"Petal..." I warn.

She shakes her head with her eyes squinted shut. "Too deep," she breathes.

"You would deny letting me fuck you the way I want?" I test, I could easily pin her hands but I want to see how far she will go to please me. She opens her eyes and slowly removes her hands from pushing me away. I push into her so fast that she screams out. A tear falls down her cheek and I lick it away as I pin her hands above her head. "There's my good girl." I fuck her hard, pounding relentlessly into her, and she takes me, takes all of me with her precious screams that fill the room. "Don't worry Petal, I'm not going to last long," I groan as her yells grow louder and I feel her pussy tighten around my cock even harder. I cum with her, needing to have her so full of me that she will always be sore. I want to be dripping out of her days from now, so that even if I am at work, she will always be thinking of me. I want to be in public, and if another man talks to her, my cum will be soaking her panties. Because she is mine, and I will mark my territory how I see fit.

"Atlas," she screams. My name on her lips doused with plea-sure, is completely blinding. Nothing will ever stop me from needing her, from needing to hear my name and the paradise it brings her.

I slowly pull out of her, knowing how sore she must feel. She brings her shaking legs down from my shoulders and I press my lips against her breathless mouth. "Mine," I say darkly.

"Yours," she pants.

I move down to her lower stomach, kissing her softly. "I can't wait for you to be carrying my child."

She pauses, controlling her breathing as she says, "what?"

"Yes Petal?" I look up to her worried expression.

"I'm on the pill," she cautiously places her fingers into my hair.

"I'm aware of that Isobel." She knows I'm psychotic enough to tamper with her birth control, and watching the fear spread across her face is getting me hard again. I can't help but smirk up at her.

"You want a baby...?"

"You could never leave then," I softly kiss her womb once more.

"I- I'm not going to leave you...did you do something to my pills?"

"And if I had?" I challenge.

She sits up, trying to distance herself from me, but I hold her firmly. "Atlas- we are fucked up...we can't bring a baby into us."

I try to hide the hurt from my face. "You think I wouldn't make a good dad?"

"That is not what I said- I just, I'm too young. And this," she gestures between us, "is a lot." I stand up from the bed, stepping back into my discarded clothing. Her eyes are full of pain as she watches me. "You're leaving?" She whispers.

"I need to run an errand for Lars."

She crosses her arms, and I can see her eyes fighting off the tears, but she has hurt me. I need some space away to process. "Something to say about that Isobel?"

"No, no. Go be a good lapdog for your brother," she turns away from me.

"What did you fucking say?"

She slowly moves her glassy eyes back to look at me. "You heard me."

I close the distance between us with two steps and reach down to grab her jaw. "I didn't do anything to your pills Isobel, but I would make a great fucking dad. I would go to the ends of the earth for my child. I would protect them like no one else could, I would keep you both safe no matter the cost." Her tears break free and I roughly let go of her jaw, grabbing my jacket, and then I storm out of her room. I can't look back, because if I do, I won't be able to leave. Not when she is crying, not when I need to punish her for this.

Not when my heart is hers to squeeze and my arteries are struggling to pump blood from her words.

How can I be fully hers if she doesn't want a baby with me?

CHAPTER TWENTY-EIGHT

ISOBEL

I cry hard the second the door slams. I have a strong urge to chase after him, but I stop myself; we both need some space. So I hug my legs to my chest and cry as the sun begins rising. At some point, the tears stop, and sleep finds me.

I wake to my phone ringing, and in my disorientation, I desperately reach for it, answering eagerly. "Iz?" My chest feels heavy from not hearing his voice.

"Bre! Hi!" I try to sound excited.

"Guess what!?"

"What?"

"I am coming tomorrow night to Devils Lake!" She squeals at the end.

"Really!?" The excitement is genuine now as I picture getting to see her again.

"What time? So Lewis and I can pick you up."

"Seven, I'm so excited to see you! And I get to meet Atlas finally."

The mention of his name causes me pain again, but I cough it away. "Yes, me too- it's just when you meet him, I just want you to know that he can seem like a lot." I figure Atlas isn't the sort of person to hide his crazy from anyone.

"What does that mean?"

"He and I are a little intense..." A lot intense, but I don't want to scare her completely.

"Okay... well, as long as you aren't fucking in front of me, I'm sure I can handle it."

"That's not what I mean- never mind, you will understand when you meet him."

"Okay, love you Iz!"

"Love you too!"

She hangs up and I look at the fire, with only a few coals left, and my ripped purple panties at the end of the bed. Why the fuck did I say all that to Atlas?

Atlas, the man that has brought me back to life.

The man who has stirred something so deep, I couldn't see the surface anymore.

The man that has killed for me.

The man that would die to keep me safe.

What the fuck did I do?

I pack a large handbag with a couple items before ringing Lewis to meet me down the front. "You wouldn't be hiding a hangover now, would you?" I tease him with his sunglasses.

"Never Isobel," his lips twitch as he opens the back door for me.

"Atlas's," I murmur as he begins driving. "You think you will be seeing that girl again?" I try to hide the smile from my face.

"Uhh no, probably not."

I shrug. "She seemed nice."

"Did you uh, did you tell Bre?"

"Would it be a problem if I did?"

"No, of course not," he coughs.

I laugh softly, "relax Lewis, I didn't tell her anything, but you are both single so I am not sure why it would be a problem."

"Yes true, she would probably just give me shit about it is all."

"Mhmm," I'm sure that's all. "Go back to bed after this Lewis, we are picking Bre up tomorrow night," I don't let him answer before I get out with my bag. His truck is out front and I have to hope that means he is home.

I open the door to him sitting at his small table, eating some food. He looks as exhausted as I feel, and part of me hopes that he was just as cut up as I was. His eyes follow me as I walk past him and empty the contents of my bag onto his bed. Then I pick up all of my loose pill packets and the box. Holding them up for him to see, I then open his wood heater and chuck them inside, and he can't stop the small smile that grabs at his lip. He pushes his chair back from the table but remains sitting. "Is this your way of apologising Petal?"

"Something like that." I have never been the greatest at apologies, and part of that is because he is also acting completely psychotic. I don't need to have a baby with him to prove that I will never leave him, but I knew how insane he was and I decided to stay. I fell in love with his crazy, and I can't just run when I don't like parts of his insane brain. So even though parts of his psycho aren't justified, I'm going to love all of him. Reason or not.

"Get on your hands and knees." I go to move onto the bed but his words stop me. "On the ground Petal." I hesitate, but do what he asks. He spreads his legs a little wider. "Crawl to me."

I go to give him a sarcastic look, but stop myself. He is punishing me for calling him a lapdog. I crawl slowly, my eyes never leaving his as I do, and then I sit between his legs, looking up at him. Patiently waiting for his next command. "Pant for me." I relax my tongue, sticking it out of my mouth before lightly panting for him. I watch as his dick gets hard against his jeans, and I press my thighs together. "Such a good bitch," he pats my head gently, unbuttoning his jeans with his other hand. Freeing his dick, I stay in character, licking from his balls all the way up to his tip, squeezing his pre-cum into my mouth.

"Mmm," I moan before taking all of him into my mouth, sucking him as his hand wraps around my hair. His breaths and soft moans encouraging me to go faster.

He rips my head up by my hair, forcing me to look at him. "If you ever call me a lapdog again, I will put a collar around your fucking neck and force you to be my pet, is that understood Petal?"

"Yes," I whisper, licking at my lips.

"I'm going to cum in your mouth, and you aren't going to waste a drop. Show me how good you suck me baby."

I do what he asks, using my hand to help my mouth, savouring the way he tastes as I watch him. He groans as I spit onto him, my eyes never leaving his as I lick and suck him with a desperation only he can fill. His grip on my nape tightens as his eyes shut and I feel his warmth pooling in my mouth. I moan as I swallow him, and then I stick my tongue out to show him I have swallowed every drop. His thumb presses against my lips, "such an obedient pet," he whispers.

I move to straddle his lap. "I'm not a pet."

He smiles before kissing me, tasting himself on my tongue. "You are whatever I want you to be Petal." He picks us up and walks us over to his bed.

"I'm sorry," I whisper. "I know you will be a great dad."

He lays us down, stroking my hair as he stares at me. "I can't wait to fill you with as many children as I want."

I inhale a deep breath. "Maybe just two?" I smile.

"A minimum of five Petal."

Jesus. "I'm sure we can compromise on that one."

He remains silent for a while, just watching me with those perfect green eyes. "My favourite colour is purple. When I was growing up, sometimes it was the only colour to light up the dark moments. These purple flowers would grow outside our trailer, and it would bring me relief from everything that was depressing."

I lightly trace the features on his face. "Thank you for sharing that with me." I kiss his nose gently, "it is a perfect colour."

He rolls on top of me, and I stroke my name on his neck. "The colour of our nursery if we have a girl?" He leaves little kisses over my face, and I giggle into his touch.

"I need to tell you something."

"Yes baby?"

"Bre is coming tomorrow night."

"I can meet her?"

"Of course, but it will also mean I need to stay at The Lodge with her for a bit." He frowns at this and I smile. "I'm sure you can handle a small amount of time apart."

"I'm sure we don't want to see how psychotic I become if you keep yourself from me."

I place my hands on either side of his face, "you are doing that thing where you are a little too dramatic."

His eyes twinkle down at me. "Want me to show you how dramatic I can be?"

"No," I smile.

"Then I'm sure Bre won't mind me sneaking in to fuck you next to her sleeping body."

I groan, "Atlas!"

"Isobel," he taunts.

"And if she wakes?"

"I can make her unconscious again," he smiles.

My eyes grow wide with fear, "you wouldn't-"

"In a safe, non-life-threatening way of course."

"You are impossible," I sigh.

"No Petal, impossible is asking me to go without you."

"You do remember I live in Chicago, and at some point, I need to go back there."

"It's like you want me to punish you," he nips at my jaw.

"Atlas, sometimes I need to spend time with Bre and my mum," I say firmly.

"Relax baby, I'm not going to keep you from them, I just love watching you all stern." I roll my eyes at him. "You seem a little tense Petal, I can fix that," he kisses down my body as his hand unbuttons my pants. "I owe you an orgasm," he says between my legs.

CHAPTER TWENTY-NINE

ISOBEL

"Y ou smell nice."

"Thanks, it's a new cologne," Lewis answers. The snow is falling enough that he has the windshield wipers on a low setting.

"Are you missing home?"

"Hmm, not really; it's more peaceful here. Do you miss it?"

"I miss mum and Bre, but I like it here," I admit.

"Only because of Atlas?"

"I guess that is a huge part of it, but I have enjoyed the slower life here." We pull in to the airport loading area, and I can see Bre waiting by her suitcase. "She's early!"

"I hope she hasn't been waiting too long in the cold," Lewis worries. Bre jumps up and down excitedly, and waves enthusiastically as she sees us pulling up. The second Lewis has pulled over, I jump out of the car and we embrace in the cold.

"Have you been waiting long?"

"Not at all, the flight was a little early, I've missed you!" She squeezes me tight again.

Lewis loads her suitcase into the trunk. "Loui!" Bre smiles.

"Bre," he offers a small smile back.

"I bet you have missed me!"

"Actually, Isobel and I were just saying how peaceful it has been."

"Well it's a good thing I have come to bring the fun then," she bats her eyelashes and I roll my eyes at them both.

"It's too soon for your bickering, let's go, it's freezing." We all jump back into the car and Lewis drives us away.

Bre hugs Lewis from behind the seat. "I bet you did miss me."

"Oh my God woman, just put your seatbelt on."

She scoffs, "so what do you think of Atlas?" She asks him as she clicks in her seatbelt.

"He uh, he is a little intense."

I can't help but smile. "Why does everyone use that word to describe him? What does it mean?"

"Isobel, would you like to explain?"

"I will when we are back in my room, okay?"

She sighs, "fine, but the suspense has been killing me."

We say goodbye to Lewis as he heads to his room and then I unlock mine.

Please do not be sitting in here waiting for me.

I exhale a breath of relief when I realise he isn't anywhere in my room, as Bre picks a spot for her luggage. Part of me was worried he wouldn't actually give us a night to catch up, and having to explain to Bre how overbearing he is with him in the room would not go down well. "This is cozy," she flops onto the bed.

"It is, but I haven't been staying here much though." I open the wood heater to put an overnight log on.

Bre has the biggest smile as her eyebrows raise. "No?" She teases.

I smile with her. "Shut up," I laugh.

"Oh I definitely won't! It has been a long time since we have been able to talk about boys."

"So let's talk, how is your love life going?"

"IZ! Stop playing hard to get and. Tell. Me. Everything."

I sit on the bed with her, "okay...but I am a little worried about your judgement."

"Iz, I would never judge you," she reaches for my hands. "I'm just so happy to see you happy," she squeezes my hands in hers. "When do I get to meet him?"

"Tomorrow," because I doubt Atlas would be okay waiting another day to see me.

She claps her hands excitedly. "Okay, and what is the sex like?"

"Bre!"

"Iz! Every goddamn detail please!"

"Fine. It is- it's world shattering."

Both of her hands immediately go to the bed as she looks at me in shock. "Go on," she whispers.

"It's unlike any sex I have ever experienced. He knows how to mix pleasure with pain- and it makes me feel alive," I admit nervously.

Her lips press together as she attempts to suppress her smile. "So are we talking like some kinky BDSM shit?"

"Uhh...maybe a little more intense than that," I pull down my tights to show her his tattoo.

She gasps, "you got tattoos together!?"

"Not quite..." I turn and face her again.

Her eyes grow big. "He tattooed you?"

"And I him," I whisper.

"Iz..."

"You said no judgement, remember?"

"I'm not, it's just- don't you think it is a little early, and now he is on you forever."

"Yes well, I thought that would be the easiest way to explain to you that we are forever."

"Pardon?"

"We are going to be together forever Bre, we know that already."

"This is what you meant about intense?"

"Yes and among other things..."

"Dear God, what else is there?"

"He is kind of psychotic..."

"Iz, at this point, you are sounding a little psychotic."

"I think we are," I look down at my fidgeting hands. "I think part of me is broken beyond repair and Atlas is the only man that I will ever feel anything with- he doesn't want to change me. I know we are fucked up, I'm not that delusional; but I love our fucked up. You don't have to like him either, but please know that he is my one chance at happiness, even if that happiness isn't normal."

She remains silent for a while, her eyes searching mine. "Does he hurt you?"

"Not in ways that I can't handle," I answer honestly.

"And you like this...?"

"I like the marks he leaves on me," my skin feels warm from her gaze.

"I'm a little conflicted."

"I knew you would be."

"He has made you happy, but it sounds like this is toxic?"

I nod my head. "It is Bre, but he would never do anything to hurt me outside of the bedroom...if that makes sense. He would do anything for me..."

"Anything?"

"Anything Bre, he protects me and makes me feel safe, something I haven't felt since..."

She squeezes my hand once more. "I understand," she says quietly.

"You do?"

"Not completely, but I will keep an open mind, I swear it."

I wrap my pinkie finger around hers. "Thankyou."

Chapter Thirty

Atlas

I wait outside the Northern Pike for Isobel, Lewis and Bre. I told her that we could go somewhere else to meet, but Isobel said she has no fear of this place with me. I smile as I think about how far she has come; she fucking loves me as much as I love her and nothing will ever change that.

I spot them walking through the carpark, Isobel's arm is linked with Bre, and they keep their heads down to avoid the light snow. Isobel is in knee-high boots, tights, and a knit dress that hugs her curves perfectly. I wonder if she wore this outfit to purposely force my hand into murder. Or maybe my Petal is just looking for a punishment. I readjust my hard dick into my waistband as I hear them both giggle over something. God, that fucking giggle makes me want to turn it into a moan, and then a scream. Preferably in that order, but I'll take any noise she gives me. One night apart is too fucking long. How can I successfully make Bre disappear without harming her? That was the question that kept me from sleeping most of last night.

Her head tilts up, and as her eyes catch me, they twinkle with the stars only I can bring her. She missed me too, that much is clear. Bre is still talking to her but I can see all of her attention has left her friend and fallen on to me. That was the problem with us, the whole fucking world could cease to exist, and we wouldn't have the faintest idea if I'm buried inside her.

And fucking hell did I want to be buried inside her.

"Atlas?" Bre asks, looking back to Isobel, who nods her head shyly. Why so shy Petal? I wonder if it's because she knows how hard I plan on fucking her later.

"Atlas this is Bre," she says quickly.

"The firecracker," I respond, to which they all look confused.

"Firecracker?" Bre asks.

"Yes, you know, after you jumped on that guy's back that was forcefully hitting on Isobel at the club," I smile. "I thought it would be a fitting name."

Bre spends a moment searching through her memories before laughing. Then she playfully hits my arm. "You told him about that?" She directs to Isobel before laughing again.

Isobel looks disarrayed before she lightly shakes her head at me and mouths 'psycho'. "Okay, well I get it now," Bre says.

"Get what?" Isobel asks confused.

"I would let this man tattoo my body also," then she stands on her tiptoes and turns my neck to the side. "The neck, really?"

"I didn't even notice that," Lewis says, smiling.

"Do you, by any chance, have a brother?" She asks and panic spreads along Lewis's face.

"You wouldn't like him," Isobel says quickly.

"What's not to like if he looks like that?" She gestures back to me.

"Drug addiction and small dick," I respond.

Bre looks genuinely disappointed as she says, "huh."

I give Lewis a quick wink, and he smiles back at me. Isobel watches us both, and her own smirk tugs at her lips. It doesn't take a fucking genius to see how much Lewis likes Bre, and maybe if I can get them both fucking, then I won't have to share my Petal with anyone.

"So, I know we all planned on eating together, but I was wondering if could get to know Atlas on my own?" Bre smiles to Isobel.

God fucking dammit.

Although, I have to give the fire cracker some credit for wanting to be alone with me. I wonder how much Isobel has told her about us. "Fine with me," I smirk.

Isobel steps toward me, "please be nice," she whispers.

Lewis and Bre have started walking inside, and I tuck my finger under her chin. "When am I ever not nice, Petal?"

"Usually when you are murdering people," she says with a smile.

"Don't joke about murder baby, you know how hard it gets me when you find it amusing."

She blushes despite the cold air. "Thank you for what you did for Lewis," she gives me a quick peck on the lips before walking away. I grab her hand and rip her back against my body.

"You wouldn't be teasing me, would you?"

"Never," she whispers as our mouths share the same breath.

"Then show me how much you missed me Petal."

She looks up to me with those dark fucking eyes before they move back to my lips, and then I lean down to kiss her, opening her mouth with my own to taste every part of her. She hums into my kiss, and I grab a fistful of her hair so that she can't escape me. Then she bites down onto my bottom lip, I wrap my hand around her neck so fast, she gasps. "Want to play Petal?"

She is breathless against my mouth. "Later," she promises.

Bre and I sit at a table four down from Isobel and Lewis, I still needed to have a view of her, and every now and then she can't resist looking at me. Bre and I both order our food and I drink, before she clears her throat. "Iz is like the most important person in my life, she's sort of vulnerable at the moment, and I guess I just want to make sure that you aren't going to hurt her." Her eyes stay on mine as she talks.

"That's not something you need to worry about Firecracker."

"Really sticking with that nickname then, Maps?"

I raise my eyebrows at her. "Really? Maps?"

She shrugs, "I think it's funny. Plus, there will be no maps on this earth that will lead to your body if you hurt her."

I laugh at her, "fair enough Firecracker, but you are wrong about something."

She looks up from her drink in question. "I think you will find I am never wrong."

I smile at her attempt at being intimidating. "Isobel isn't vulnerable. She is fucking strong. No man could ever break her, certainly not me."

Her eyes go glassy for a moment, but she composes herself. "I take it back; I can be wrong." A man approaches Isobel and Lewis's table, and I find myself clenching the edge of our own. He says something to her, and Isobel shakes her head. Then he reaches down to touch her cheek, and she flinches out of his touch.

"Excuse me for a second," I tell Bre as I walk over to him with a blind rage. The kind of rage that has me murdering first and asking questions never. Isobel's eyes get big when she sees me coming, and before the guy can even turn around to see me, I grab the back of his head and smash his face against their table, Lewis jumps in shock. The guy's body drops to the ground, and without saying a word, I drag him away from them; leaving his unconscious body by the bar. Most people here know me well enough not to question my outbursts.

I head back to my table, sliding into my chair. "Sorry, where were we?"

"You are psychotic," Bre murmurs.

I hold up my finger and thumb in a small pinch gesture. "Just a tiny bit, nothing to concern yourself about."

"I would say broken faces are quite concerning Maps."

"Oh Firecracker, you should see what I can do with a cleaver."

"I'm not entirely sure whether I should take Iz far away from you, or if you should marry her."

"Well, the second option would be the safest."

"You're not going to let anyone hurt her ever again, are you?"

"They would be dead before they could even try."

Slowly, a smile spreads across her face. "I like you Maps."

"A mutual feeling then, Firecracker," and she clinks her drink against mine.

CHAPTER THIRTY-ONE

ISOBEL

"Part of me is thankful that Atlas did that, so that I didn't have to. Then another part of me is like he needs to calm the fuck down," Lewis says as he picks up the cutlery that was knocked from our table.

"I um, don't think Atlas knows how to calm the fuck down."

"Protective much," he wipes his fork with his napkin.

"You don't even know the half of it."

The unconscious guy eventually comes to, he is greeted with a shot of whiskey and an icepack from the bartender. Atlas has this whole town terrified of him, has the people not questioning his choices. Nobody in this place bothered to help that man until he came to, and the man made no attempt to go anywhere near Atlas. He is feared, and ruthless, and all mine. Him being mine made me realise something so crucial for me; I am now feared as well. My first night here resulted in multiple guys hitting on me, girls stealing from me, and my second night was even more terrifying, but now I am the terror. The men now go out of their way to avoid staring at me. I am invincible; and I am free.

Free from the fear that has haunted my every movement since my cousin's abuse, free from looking over my shoulder because I know that Atlas is behind me, and nothing is scarier than him. If the price for this freedom was selling my soul to the devil, I would sign with my own blood, and kneel before him every goddamn day.

Lewis and I move to some barstools surrounding a small high table in the corner, and eventually Bre joins us. "Maps and I are practically besties," she smiles as she slides onto a stool beside Lewis.

"Maps?" Lewis asks, confused.

"My nickname for her psychotic boyfriend."

"Where is he?" I turn my head to look.

"His brother wanted to talk to him. It's a shame about the small dick thing, because damn, he is hot."

Lewis chokes on his drink, and I smile. "A shame indeed," I answer.

"Maybe I could look past it, because Iz! We would truly be sisters then!"

"We already are sisters, and don't forget about the drug issue."

She sighs, "true."

"So you really got along?"

"He is intense- like you said, and I think you need intense Iz," Bre doesn't elaborate with Lewis around, and I'm grateful for that. Lewis knowing what happened to me, isn't really something I want; I would hate the sympathy that would fill his eyes every time we spoke.

"Lewis!" A girl's voice calls.

"Oh no," Lewis whispers.

Bre and I both turn our heads; it is the girl he hooked up with the other night. *Oh shit.*

Lewis stands up to greet the girl who throws her arms around his neck, we can't hear what they are saying as he talks to her. "Who is that?" Bre asks, her face has scrunched up as she attempts not to watch them.

"Uhh, just this girl he met the other night."

"Why didn't he tell me he was seeing someone?"

"I think it was more of a one-night thing."

"Oh," she slides the straw of her drink into her mouth. "Did he say much about her?"

"No Bre, you wouldn't be jealous, would you?"

She scoffs, "of Loui? Of course not."

I shrug, "I mean he's hot, he is going to get attention."

"You think he's hot?"

"Just because I have been turned off from all men besides Atlas, doesn't mean I am blind."

She shrugs and looks back at her drink, she is most definitely jealous. For some time now, I couldn't work out if Bre liked Lewis back. I knew she liked his reactions to her, but now I can see it goes further than that. Lewis comes back over to us, and with Bre already a few drinks deep, I know exactly how this will end.

"Leeewwwiiissss," Bre exaggeratedly mimics the girl.

"Don't even start," he warns.

"Oh no, me? Never...I was just going to say that she looks like a respectable young lady, you know? The kind you take home to mummy dearest."

Something flashes in Lewis's eyes, not the passive look he wears around Bre to shut up her up as quickly as possible, but something like a challenge dances there. "I wasn't really looking for respectable," he smiles.

Let the bickering begin.

Bre is taken off guard by his response, and her cheeks turn pink under the warm white lights. She attempts to act like she doesn't care, checking her nails as she responds, "I just didn't realise your standards were so low."

"You want to talk standards? I have driven home some of the men you let in your sheets."

She gasps, "well at least those guys didn't have their asses hanging out in the middle of winter!"

"Bre, if you want to say you are jealous, just say it."

At this point I would kill for some popcorn. I imagine Atlas on a murdering rampage to get me my popcorn, and I can't help but let out a little giggle. Bre flashes me a stare colder than death, she stands up, attempting to seem more intimidating; but Lewis still towers over her.

"Jealous of you Loui? You would have to be joking- you would have to be mad! I would N.E.V.E.R be jealous of you. In fact-"

"Shut up," Lewis says calmly.

"Excuse you!? You can't-"

Lewis cuts off Bre's words with his mouth, smashing his lips against hers violently. *OH SHIT!* I thought I had this ending planned out, but now I have been hit with a twist. They break away for a moment. "I said shut up," he says against her mouth and she nods her head as he kisses her more, walking her body to the back wall.

Time for me to leave, I slip away, letting them have their moment; but I can't stop smiling. This is actually happening. I head for the bathroom before I go looking for Atlas and Lars. Thankfully, there is no one in here, not that I need to worry now that I am with Atlas. I flush my wee, and all the toilet paper I used to cover the seat, just as I am about to leave my stall; I hear the bathroom door creak open. *Damn it.*

Maybe I'll just wait in here until they are gone, but then I hear the door locking and the lights are turned off. Fear encircles around my legs and begins rising through my body. Then slow, taunting footsteps begin to walk along the tiles. "Hello?" I call out, but my tone falters and the fear cracks through. There is no answer, but I hear the footsteps stop outside my stall. "Atlas?" I whisper fearfully.

The door shakes and I yelp, moving back, but I can't see a fucking thing. "This isn't funny..."

"Ready to play Petal?"

"I am going to murder you," the tingling sensation of adrenalin spreads along my skin.

"Is that a joke or a threat? Either way, I am hard baby."

"Unfortunately, there is a locked door in your way," I tease.

"You think a door could stop me taking what is mine?"

I quietly step up onto the toilet. "I guess you better come and get me."

I get ready to hoist myself over the other stall the moment he kicks the door down. My heart is pounding fiercely with our little game. There is a loud smash, and I push my body up, swinging my legs over the divider. I quietly go to jump over, as my body falls; his arms catch me. I scream before giggling, kicking in his arms as he holds me tight. "You can never escape me Petal."

I relax in his strong arms, "I never want to Atlas. I would only ever run knowing you would catch me."

He carries me out of the stall, turning me around so that my back is pressed against his chest. "I am going to bend you over this sink and fuck you like you deserve."

"Like I deserve?" I ask, already breathless.

"Nothing more than a whore being fucked in a public bathroom, desperate for everyone outside to hear how good I fuck you."

"Your whore," I whisper.

"Yes, only mine. My good little whore that will let me fuck her wherever I want."

He bends me over and my hands find the sink, then he rips my tights and bunches up my dress. His hands move to grip my ass, his fingers sliding to my pussy, and he groans. "Crotchless panties, Petal? You really were just begging to get fucked." I hear him spit into his hand and then he is rubbing his warmth around my entrance. "Such a good whore for me."

"Please," I groan, needing him to stretch and fill me. He pushes inside me, and I grip the sink tighter. "Atlas," I moan.

"God, always so fucking tight," his fingers dig roughly into my skin as he thrusts inside me. I push back against him, matching his rhythm as my moans grow louder. He rips me up by my hair, "so loud for my cock, Petal. Does it turn you on knowing people can hear?"

"Yes," I breathe, and he drops my hair, fucking me hard as my moans turn to screams.

"Cum for me, my little whore."

My core tenses and then the orgasm ripples through me, causing my legs to feel heavy. Atlas follows after me, groaning as he comes inside me. I lean breathlessly against the sink as Atlas moves to turn on the lights. I squint as my eyes adjust to the brightness, and force my shaking legs to turn around as he rips the rest of my tights away, discarding them in the bin. Then he gently presses his lips against mine. "Perfect," he whispers.

I go to head into the stall to clean up his cum, but he grabs me by my hand. "Don't clean yourself up, I want my cum running down your legs baby."

Chapter Thirty-two

Isobel

I wake to my head pounding viciously. Even opening my eyes to the light hurts me. I stumble out of bed for my bag. Atlas must already be gone to work. I pull out two painkillers and down them with my water. A slickness forms between my legs, and at first, I think it must just be Atlas's cum, but once I look down, I see the blood. I groan, now it makes sense. Why is this so hard? I stumble back to bed with my eyes shut, begging for the pain relief to come. When my headache begins to subside, I put Atlas's sheets in the wash and have a shower, sitting in there to help with my cramps. Then I realise that this is my first period off of birth control in six years.

This fucking sucks.

Thanks to my psychotic boyfriend, I now have to deal with this shitty period all because he is insane. I hope it rains instead of snows while he is working outside. Then I hope that his coffee is cold and his lunch is off. I smile as I realise the best punishment for him will be no sex for a week. I grab one of his shirts and my own track pants, before hopping back into bed. Just as my eyes feel heavy, my phone dings. I groan loudly, reaching to see who could possibly be disturbing me.

Bre
Be there soon, Lewis is dropping me off.

Bring Turkish delights.

Bre
Period?

HURRY WITH SNACKS.

Sorry, that was my period. Xo

Bre comes with a greasy bacon and egg roll, a box of Turkish delights, and a milkshake. "You are the best," I say as I stuff my mouth with grease.

"Why is this period so shit? Have you skipped too many with your pill?"

"No judgement?"

"Okay...I won't."

"Because I emotionally don't think I could handle it right now."

She laughs before biting into her own roll. "Just tell me."

"I stopped taking the pill."

"To try a different birth control?"

"No..."

"So you are on no birth control?"

"Correct," I sip my shake.

"And you are having more sex than you have ever had in your life?"

"Also correct."

She presses her lips together in frustration. "Would this be Maps' idea?"

"Yes."

"And what is his reasoning for wanting you to be a mother at the ripe old age of twenty-two?"

"So I can never leave him."

"Have you tried telling him that you won't leave as a less drastic option?"

"I can confirm that I tried that first."

"Right. Unsuccessful?"

"Yes, hence this shitty period."

"Do you want to be a mother?"

I realise that this is something we have never talked about, I guess because of our young age it has never really crossed our minds. "I want a family with him," I say honestly. She sighs. "You are struggling to withhold your judgement?"

"Well yes, but I will just say this instead; I will make a killer aunty."

I smile, "you certainly will, now. Enough about me, tell me about last night!?"

"It was...unexpected."

"Was it?" I ask, raising my eyebrows.

"I think a part of me always felt something for him, but I never thought it was that strong until I saw that girl wrap her arms around his neck."

"Was it awkward this morning?" Sometimes things can seem different the next day with no alcohol involved.

"I woke him up with a blowjob."

"Oh...so not awkward?"

She smiles, "I just need to say this...he knows how to fuck."

"Bre!" Hearing that kind of feels like hearing something about my brother now.

"And he has a massive dick, I don't know why he acts all shy with a dick that big."

"Oh my god Bre!" I cover my ears, but she pulls my hands away.

"Iz, you wanted to know! Plus, he has some stamina, I'm talking three times last night and twice this morning."

"Jesus..."

"We are going on a proper date tonight, so I hope you don't need his driving services."

"Of course not, I do not feel like leaving this bed all week."

"Excellent! Catch up tomorrow so I can give you all the details?"

"Maybe some slight fewer details next time."

Bre leaves, and between turning his sheets over by the fire to get them dry, and scrolling socials for a while, I fall to sleep. My headache is back when I wake, and I take some more painkillers, as I look at his dry bedsheets. The thought of having to make his bed right now feels impossible. I feel like I could sleep for this entire period and only wake up for Turkish Delights.

I see Atlas's headlights pull up and I realise I have barely moved all day. I lay cuddled with his blanket tightly around me, and I am yet to make the bed still. He walks inside, hanging his jacket immediately. "Petal?"

"Hey."

He walks over to me, "what no run and jump into my arms tonight?"

"No."

There is a small tug of his lips and my anger bubbles further. "Is something wrong?"

I shrug.

"Isobel, either you can tell me what's going on or I am going to fix that attitude right now."

"I got my period."

"Oh, I'm sorry?"

"You should be. It's your fault. This is my first period since stopping the pill and it sucks!" He is fighting off a smile. "If you make fun of me right now, I will actually murder you."

"Oh baby..." But he can't stop the smile spreading.

"Don't oh baby me! I bled all over your sheets, my head is pounding and my cramps are stabbing my uterus in two." He chews on the side of his thumb, attempting to hold back laughter now. "All because you are a psychotic psycho!"

"Psychotic psycho?"

"Don't!" I point aggressively, warning him not to make fun of me.

"What was my punishment?" he diverts.

I shrug, "there were a few options, but I decided on my favourite."

"Please do tell Petal."

"We can't have sex now for a week."

He tilts his head back and laughs, laughs louder than I have ever heard from him before. "Oh Petal, you just provided our lube for the week," he smiles mischievously. I cross my arms and death stare him. "I will be back in a minute. Stay in this little cocoon and watch American Horror Story," he grabs his jacket, keys, and wallet.

"How do you know I love that show?" He just gives me a look as if to say, really? I wave my hand. "Right, psychotic and all."

Atlas comes back fifteen minutes later with a bag fall of stuff and a bunch of purple carnations; he places the bag on his kitchen cupboard before coming over to me. Without saying a word, he scoops me into his arms and places me on a seat by the fire, still wrapped up in his blanket. Then he makes his bed as I silently watch. He comes back to pick me up, carrying me back to his bed and tucking me under his sheets. He kisses my forehead before fluffing the blanket back over me. Then he puts the flowers in a glass of water beside me. "Where are you going?" I whisper.

He walks back to the kitchen, "to cook you steak and broccoli, you need red meat. Then I will make a banana split for dessert. Bananas help with period cramps. I also replaced the box of Turkish Delights you seem to have eaten all today."

He cooks for me, bringing me my steak in bed, then he makes dessert and hops into bed with me, watching my comfort show together. I am so fucking in love with this man that I don't know how to handle it. I feel like I will combust at any moment from loving him too fiercely. "Thank you," I whisper into his chest.

"I will always take care of you Petal." I attempt to fight off my hormonal tears as the episode finishes. "You know, I have heard that sex can help period cramps," his hand moves under my shirt, lightly grazing my nipples.

I roll my eyes, "have you?"

"Yes. It's science."

"Was this scientist a man?"

He pinches my nipple, and I arch into his touch. "I mean, it's the least I can do after I forced this period upon you. Let me take away your pain Petal, and bring you the kind you like." He moves his head down and places my nipple into his mouth, licking and sucking before he gently bites. I moan and grab his hair. He tugs my sweatpants down, and I help by arching up my hips.

"Atlas- I have never done this before. Could we maybe turn the light off?" He has his hands on my period underwear.

"Absolutely not Petal." He pulls my underwear down, discarding them on the floor, and I cover my face with my hands. "If you want to hide from me, then you can get on all fours."

I swallow nervously. "Now," he says sternly. I do what he asks, turning around on my hands and knees, and wait patiently as he takes off his pants. The mattress shifts and then he is behind me, gripping my ass as he begins to push inside me. "Fuck," he groans.

I exhale a deep breath, letting my head fall to his bed, relishing the way he fills me. "That does feel really good," I moan.

"There's so much blood," he whispers, slowly pulling out and back in to me.

"I-I'm sorry."

"I fucking love it, seeing my dick coated in your blood is stirring something primal in me."

I push back against him, loving the sounds our bodies make when they meet. I hear him reaching into his bedside drawer. "What are you doing?"

"I need to fuck your ass Petal; I can't wait any longer." He squirts liquid over me, rubbing it around before sliding two fingers deep inside me.

I grip the sheets tighter. "Atlas," I moan.

"You like me in your tight little ass, don't you?"

Oh god. "Yes," I push back on him, forcing him to go faster.

He withdraws his cock and his fingers, and I whimper from the loss of him. He squirts more lube around me and onto himself before the tip of his cock is at my ass. "This is going to hurt Petal, but I promise you will end up loving it."

Slowly he starts to stretch me and gone is the enjoyable feeling of his fingers. He has replaced that with a pain so strong; I feel like he will tear me apart. "Atlas-" I panic.

"It's okay," he groans, still pushing deeper into me.

Tears spring to my eyes as I attempt to get away from him, but he holds me firmly in place. "It hurts." A sob leaves my throat.

"I know baby, I know. You are taking me so well though," he slides slowly further.

"I can't do this Atlas," a few tears fall down my cheeks.

"I'm going to hurt with you baby," he stills his movements as he reaches for his bedside table again. He hisses, and I feel warm droplets fall onto my back.

"What is that?"

"My blood Petal," then he pushes all the way into my ass and I cry out. "Holy fuck, this feels too good," slowly he thrusts into me.

"Atlas," I moan. "I- I want you to go harder."

"Are you sure?"

I slam back against him, moaning loudly as he groans his approval. "You like it, baby?"

"I fucking love it."

"See how good you are Petal, I get to be the first and only man to fill your ass with my cum."

"Please," I beg, and he pumps into me so fast that I can't do anything but take it.

"Fuck, Isobel!" He slows his thrusts before ever so gently pulling out of me. I feel his cum pooling out of my ass as I flop to the bed. "Are you sore baby?"

I nod my head, and he leaves into the bathroom, coming back with a wet towel. He wipes me down softly, and I wince as he wipes over my ass. "You took me so fucking well baby."

I slowly sit up. "What did you do to yourself?" I search his body as I remember the blood that dripped onto my back. Taking up his entire left forearm is the word Petal, carved into his skin with a knife.

CHAPTER THIRTY-THREE

ISOBEL

A month went by of falling into Atlas's psychotic rhythm. Bre went back to Chicago two weeks ago, and Lewis and I are both struggling without her. I nervously pace Atlas's small trailer as I wait for him to get home from work. It has been on my mind for some time now, what I want to say to him, but it still terrifies me. Tonight is the night, and I will not back down. I have his favourite meal cooked for him, which is my homemade lasagne, and I also made a sticky date pudding. I'm wearing nothing but his shirt because I know how crazy that makes him, and I also cleaned his home.

Nothing will go wrong.

His truck pulls up and the butterflies in my stomach aggressively flap around. I take some steadying breaths as he walks through the door and I shyly greet him. "You made lasagne!?"

I smile, "yes."

He kisses me as he slides off his jacket. "I need to taste all of you first Petal."

"Before we do that- I, um, need to talk to you about something."

A flicker of fear flashes quickly across his face. "Is it something that will cause me to feel murderous?"

"Come sit," I lead him to our table. My heart swells at the realisation that his home is actually ours. "I need to go back to Chicago." His eyes darken and he goes to protest, but I hold up my hand for him to wait. "I desperately need to see my mum. I need to convince her and Bre to move back here for good, and I need to clear out my home." His eyes light up like I have never seen before. "I want to be with you forever Atlas," my pace quickens with my nerves. "I want my family here so that I never need to leave you again, and I want you to stop working. I want you to come work for me, maybe as my bodyguard? So that when I go on book tours, we never have to be apart." I exhale a long breath, "if that is what you want..."

"Baby, why would you be nervous about telling me this?"

"Because...it hasn't been that long that this all started," I gesture between us.

He smiles, "time is immeasurable for us, Petal."

"I love you, Atlas."

"I love you," he reaches for my hand, kissing the back of it.

"After dinner, I need to go back to The Lodge to pack, because I leave first thing in the morning." He goes to argue that, but I quickly jump in, "and when I get home, we can build our dream house together."

He inhales a deep breath, "okay," he smiles.

"Okay," I smile back.

With my room packed and ready to go, I decide that there is no way I can spend tonight without Atlas. I reach for the keys, leaving Lewis in peace for tonight. He is beyond ecstatic to be seeing Bre again, and he told me they would be face timing tonight. As I go to head out the door, Mum starts ringing me. I sit back on my bed as I answer. "Mum?"

"Hi darling, how are you going?"

"All packed, and excited to see you again," this is the longest I have ever been without my mum.

"Me too sweetie, I needed to talk to you about something."

"Is everything okay?" Worry settles in my throat with her tone.

"Yes- it's just your uncle called me," my blood goes cold at the mention of him. "He wanted me to pass on the message that he is having a funeral for Micheal and your father."

I have no idea why, but I never expected this. "But they haven't found them...?"

"Your uncle says he knows that they are gone, and that he wants to honour their memory by finally saying a proper goodbye."

Well, I honoured Micheal's memory by getting fingered over his death.

"But Dad isn't dead..." I know Micheal is, but I can't say this out loud, but Micheal and my dad's disappearance have nothing in common, even though everyone else thinks they do. I however, know the truth that can never be told.

"I know how hard this is to accept Isobel, but I think we should both go." Suddenly, the abyss that I have been blissfully drowning in opens up. The room feels like it is swaying around me as I try to focus on my breathing. Everything blends together in my brain as I realise there is one very important factor that I have continued to look over. One single common anomaly to both of their disappearances. Atlas was at the same place they were when they disappeared.

"Mum- I need to call you back," I hang up immediately. Lars said he remembered seeing him- Lars, Atlas's brother, the only person in this fucking town to have seen him. My breathing becomes erratic as I grab my keys, holding my straining heart in my chest as I head for the car.

This cannot be real. This cannot be real.

I drive faster than I should to his trailer, feeling the breaths begin to consume my entire body- panicking that I will pass out before I even get to his. I run up his steps, still clutching my chest as I open his door. He rushes to me, "Petal?"

I can't stop the heavy breaths enough to talk. His face and eyes go to a very dark place. "What happened?" He demands, ready to murder the entire world for me.

My hands shake in front of me as I take in a deep, steadying breath. "What did you do to my father?"

Chapter Thirty-four

Atlas

Fuck.

The terror and realisation in her eyes destroy me.

She knows.

I don't know how, but she does. "Isobel-" I reach for her, but she rips herself away.

"Don't! Tell me what- tell me what you did, Atlas," her eyes water with tears, and I feel my own threatening to come.

"Okay, I will tell you everything, please just come sit." I hold my hand out for her to sit on the edge of my bed.

She does what I ask, mainly because she is shaking so much, she is probably struggling to stand. I grab a chair and sit opposite her, but I don't attempt to reach for her this time. "I will tell you the complete truth, but I need you to know that we are real baby," her eyes dart up to mine and there is nothing but coldness there. I swallow at my pained throat. "Your dad was an addict." Her eyes flicker with pain. "I'm not sure if you knew this or not, but he owed many people money, and continued to drive farther to find his fix. He found Lars, who gave him drugs. Your dad came back to him the following night for more; but hadn't paid." She blinks away her tears, and it causes me physical pain not to taste them.

"It got heated between them both because your dad was desperate for more, and Lars- he killed him baby."

She sobs loudly. "How?"

"Petal...you don't need to know that."

"H.O.W."

"A hammer to the head."

She cries, bending forward as she sobs, and I need to hurt with her- I need for our pain to be combined. "Where do you come into this?" She sniffs, wiping at her tears.

I suck in a shaky breath. "I disposed of his body."

She gets up abruptly, rushing for the bathroom. The sound of her vomiting causes me even more pain. Cautiously, I follow her. She rinses her mouth before coming to the doorway where I am waiting. "Petal..."

"NO!" She screams. "I-" her words are being choked on her shock, her wide eyes completely terrified of me, and this time it doesn't stir anything down to my dick; this time her fear only scares me. "You are dead to me Atlas."

She walks past me, and her words are far stronger than any bullet. "Petal-" I panic following her.

She whirls around, "you knew this entire time!" Her tears come back, "I came to this town to find my father, and I ended up fucking the man that buried him!"

"I wanted to tell you, please baby-" I reach for her but she shoves me away. I drop to my knees for her, and she sobs again.

Kneeling for the first time for somebody other than him.

"Please Isobel- I never meant to love you, I never meant for any of this," I wrap my arms around her legs. "I can't live without you baby, my soul couldn't take it," she shakes with her tears. I start making my way up her body, until her face is between my hands. I wipe at her tears as my own fall down my face. "Please baby, tell me what I can do to make this right- anything Isobel, I will do anything."

"Bleed for me," she chokes out.

"Done." I reach for my knife, holding it in my hand. "How much?"

She composes herself, wrapping her hand around mine; causing the blade to dig into my palm. I don't flinch as the blood pools in our hands. "All of it," she says with dead eyes. The same eyes she used on her attackers, and then she leaves.

"FUCK!!!!!" I scream, throwing the knife. It isn't enough, and I begin to throw everything in sight, destroying my home, because this place is nothing without her. I am nothing without her.

I punch and throw until my knuckles are coated in blood. She just needs some time, I begin pacing. Time to process, time to forgive me. I- I need to give her space, she will come around, she has to. And if she doesn't- I will just have to kidnap her. There is no other option. I will force her to love me again, no matter how long it takes, no matter how long I need to keep her locked up. She will be mine.

I need to let her go back to Chicago, give her a small amount of space, let her realise that her soul also couldn't survive without me, and then take her. I can do that, I can wait. It's better this way, no secrets between us now. No secrets ever again.

I work at calming my mind as my chest aches. We were so close to having it all, so close to a life I never thought possible for myself. My racing thoughts stop me from hearing a car rock up, and before I have time to process that someone is here; Lars walks in. "Atlas?" He steps in, taking in my trashed home. "What the fuck happened?"

I start to clean up my place, "I left Isobel," I lie.

He whistles, "that must have been hard...but it's for the best Atlas. Fucking the girl of the dad we murdered was dark even for you, brother."

"You murdered," I correct.

He laughs, "and if I didn't, you would have eventually; if he never paid us."

"Do you have a job for me?" I partly wanted him to say yes, just so I could go break some bones. The clean snapping noise always seemed to calm me.

"No, I just came to hang out."

"I'm not great company right now."

He picks up a chair, bringing it back over to my table. "I'm here for you, want to get high?"

"No."

"Drunk?"

"No."

"Set someone's house on fire?"

The last one was actually tempting. "No, I think I just want to be alone and clean up. How about I come see you tomorrow?"

Lars comes over and slaps my shoulder, "you did the right thing brother, no loose ends right?"

"Right," I give him a fake smile, hopefully selling to him that I will be fine on my own.

"See you tomorrow," and then he leaves.

How long is an appropriate amount of time to let her miss me? I wasn't sure I had anything longer than a week in me, two weeks at the absolute max. I continue to tidy my mess as I begin planning how I will keep her as mine. The fact that she is a public figure will definitely make this more challenging, but I'm not above leaving the States with her. Starting somewhere entirely fresh for the both of us. Two weeks to plan every little detail I will need to pull this off, and after; she will never leave me again.

After finally getting my house back in order, and repairing some of the wooden items I destroyed, my phone chimes, I rush to it; hoping to see her name flash on the screen. It is Lewis, and he has sent me a message only saying LA.

LA? Is he trying to hint to me where Isobel will be running off to?

Trying to give me a heads up so that I can find them? I go start replying, but then my hands begin to shake- Lars.

No loose ends.

Chapter Thirty-five

Isobel

I brush my teeth and then splash water onto my red face. My eyes are swollen from all the tears, and a headache has started throbbing above my eyebrows. How could I be this stupid? I knew after my cousin that trusting a man would be impossible.

Lewis is waiting for me in the car, he doesn't know exactly what happened, but he knows it is bad enough for me to want to leave tonight. I just needed a minute, some time to collect my emotions before I leave.

Atlas has betrayed me, more than I could ever imagine. He knew, this entire time, he talked about him with me, watched me ask others if they had seen him. He lied straight to my face and then carved his name into my soul without ever thinking of the consequences. Did he even care? I know he cares about me, but did it plague his sleep at night, keeping this from me? Or would he have gone forever with me and never said a word, let me spend my whole life wondering what happened to him? The tears threaten to spill over again, but I control myself. "Enough," I whisper.

I grab my toothbrush and paste, heading out of the bathroom. I needed my mum's cuddles, and that was the only thing that would come close to healing everything he has destroyed. He saved me, only to rip every piece of me away again. I will never touch another man as long as I live, vibrators will be it from now on. I would have to change my whole life. I know he will come after me, know that his threats are never empty. Now I would be forcing Mum, Bre, and Lewis into hiding with me. Having the amount of money I do means that I can find a way to hide from him, but my life will always involve me looking over my shoulder now.

I sigh and step out of the bathroom; Lars is waiting by my bed. I stop dead in my tracks, frozen with confusion and fear. "Izzy," he smiles darkly.

"What are you doing here?" My voice cracks from all the crying.

"Well, I went to see my dear brother, he is quite torn up about you breaking up."

"He told you?" I whisper.

"He told me he broke things off with you, but I know Atlas. He would never leave you, which left me realising that there would only be one possible reason for you to leave him. That you discovered the truth." He begins walking closer to me, and I fight with everything to control my fear. "So Izzy, this is nothing personal, but no loose ends I'm afraid." Just as he goes to grab me, I jab my fist as hard as I can into his throat. He coughs and I run around him, only for him to rip me back by my hair. My body falls to the ground, as he places his on top of mine. "Well, now it is personal," he wraps his hands around my throat, his eyes lighting up with the utter desperation I feel.

"Lars-" I choke out, clawing at his hands, thrashing my legs as hard as I can, hoping I get lucky and knee him between his legs. My throat makes gurgling noises as the world around me begins to feel light. I can feel his dick hard against my thigh as he continues to choke me. He is getting off on killing me. This is how I will die, with a man's unwanted erection pressing into me, the last of my tears fall from my eyes as the darkness comes for me.

Just before everything goes completely dark, Lars is ripped away from me. I choke the air back into my body, on my hands and knees, I cough life back into me. "I will fucking kill you!" I look up to Atlas blocking Lars from me.

"I know you would have been mad at me for a while brother, but she needs to die. You know it, I know it, you really think she will keep your secret now that she hates you?"

I still gasp for air as I work my body on getting farther away from them. "She is off limits. Forever Lars."

Lars sighs, "I'm sorry to have to do this Atlas," he pulls out a gun. "But you can't hate me forever, she on the other hand, will hate us forever now."

He goes to pull the trigger; I hear Atlas scream as he rushes to protect my body with his. The gun doesn't sound loud when it is fired, and I assume Lars has silenced it. The bullet hits Atlas in the arm, and he moves so fast, disabling the gun from Lars. In amongst their fighting, the gun is skidded over to me. I rush to grab it, Atlas has Lars pinned beneath him, punching him as Lars works to get free. "Fuck you!" Atlas yells.

"Fuck you for making me do this," I watch as he quickly pulls out his knife. His hand shakes as he works to use it, as he battles with himself, with his own brother to finish the deed.

"Atlas-"

Before Lars can finish his sentence, Atlas lodges the knife into his throat. There are horrible gurgling and spluttering noises as Lars suffocates on the blood flowing from his neck. With shaking hands, I raise the gun to Atlas, to the man that buried my father, to the man that betrayed me deeper than anyone ever could. My finger nervously taps on the trigger as he lets out a scream.

"FUCK!!!!!!" He cries, his bloodied hands covering his face as his haunted sobs fill my room. My heart cracks in two with his pain. The gun drops from my hands as I process what has happened.

He killed his own brother for me.

Blood for blood, flesh for flesh, a body for a body; Atlas repaid a debt I didn't know needed settling. My father for his brother, he took away the one family he has left for me. Killed the only person that truly saw what he dealt with, who fought those demons alongside of him; and now he cries, broken in his brother's blood.

I rush to him, dropping beside him as the warmth from Lars's blood soaks into my pants. "Hey," I whisper, reaching for his head, but he shoves me away. He can't look at me as his wet face only focuses on the knife sticking out of Lars's throat. "Atlas," I reach for him again, he doesn't push me away, but he still won't look at me. "Atlas," I soothe, my hand on his bloodied cheek. "We are going to have a baby," I whisper.

Slowly, his eyes turn to mine. "What?" He chokes out.

I nod my head nervously. "I'm pregnant."

"Wh-why didn't you tell me?"

"It is really early; I was going to surprise you when I came back from Chicago."

His whole body turns to me now, and he places a hand on my lower stomach. "You're pregnant?" He breathes.

I smile now. "I'm pregnant."

His lips crash against mine, claiming me as I moan into his open mouth. He begins undressing me, but I reach for his arm. "Atlas, you're bleeding."

"Later," he murmurs against my mouth and carries me to my bed, sitting on the edge as he lowers me onto him. He has to stop to rub some spit around so that he can slide inside me easier.

"Oh god," I moan out. Lars's blood is smudged along our skin as we both desperately touch each other everywhere. Atlas's lips only leave mine to move down my neck. He keeps one hand wrapped around me, holding me as I fuck him; and he moves the other back to my stomach.

"We will be better," he whispers against my mouth. "We will create a family where cousins and brothers don't hurt each other."

"Atlas," I moan.

He keeps his hand on my stomach, the blood from his bullet wound trickling down, coating us further in blood. "I will keep you both safe forever, Petal."

"Forever," and then I cum, digging my nails into his arm as my hips jolt against him. He follows shortly after; I kiss his groans while he finishes inside me.

I rest my forehead against his as our breathing becomes softer. "Lewis!" I think in a panic.

"He is okay, Lars knocked him out, but he is alive- he messaged me Isobel, saved your life. Saved our life," he corrects. Because there is no world for us now if the other is gone. "I think Lars was expecting me to finish him off once you were gone."

"Your arm," I worry as the blood still drips from his fingers.

"I need you to check if the bullet is still in there for me."

With shaking hands, I look at his wound. "Yes," I whisper.

"Do you have tweezers?"

"Yes." I pour out the contents of my hygiene bag. I come back to him holding the tweezers, "got them."

"I need you to pull the bullet out."

"I don't know how- we need to get you to a hospital."

"Baby, we can't go to a hospital, you can do it."

"Isn't this going to contaminate the crime scene?"

"Petal, we just fucked on the crime scene, and there will be no crime scene soon, I just need you to get the bullet out."

"Okay," I whisper. Moving my hands to his wound, I flinch as I shove the tweezers into his open arm. Atlas doesn't make a noise as I feel the tweezers latch on to the bullet. "Got it."

"Good job baby, now pull it out."

"Doesn't it hurt?"

"Very much so," but he still doesn't flinch or make a sound as I pull it out, more blood coming with it. Then he rips the bottom part of my shirt, handing it for me to use as a bandage. "Make it tight Petal."

After I finish tying his makeshift bandage, I begin to shake as my head looks back to Lars's lifeless eyes, to the blood that has emptied his limp body. "Wh-what do we do?" I whisper, my shaking growing.

"I will take care of it all baby," he dresses me. "Go, take Lewis to my trailer, I will fix this."

"How?" I ask, more tears trailing down my cheeks.

"Tish can hack the cameras; I will deal with the clean-up. Go Petal, you are going in to shock."

"I- I can't leave you alone in this," I protest, but looking at his body is making me queasy.

Atlas places a hand on my cheek, "I am okay baby, I need to know that you two are safe, I will be home as soon as I can. Ice Lewis's head, okay?"

"Okay," I whisper, and he kisses me softly.

"There is no undoing our souls now, we are bounded for life Petal, darkness and all."

CHAPTER THIRTY-SIX

ISOBEL

Two and a half years later

We drive through the trees and cliff side, the lake follows us, the warm sun reflecting off it as we drive. Atlas's hand rests on my thigh, and my hand rests on his. "Oh no," I whisper.

Atlas turns his direction to our son in the back. "He's sleeping," he sighs.

"Now we will be dealing with a late bedtime," I groan.

"That was when I planned on playing with you," his hand trails further up my thigh.

"You always manage to do both, anyway." We pass a house that just has the wooden skeleton up. "Mum and Jacks?"

"Yes Petal," he confirms. "It's really just us out here, isn't it?" My gaze wanders back to the sparkling lake. I convinced Mum to move here, and she ended up finding a lumberjack of her own, funny that his name is actually Jack. Bre and Lewis brought a house here in Devils Lake also, and together we have all become a family. "Oh my..."

We pull up to a large two-story beige stone home, with dark wood and large windows. "Atlas-" I don't even have the words, as I take in our incredible view of the lake and trees.

"Is it what you imagined?" He asks nervously.

"So much more," I squeeze his hand reassuringly. He built this home for us, designed it all himself, and built it alongside other builders. "Are you getting the little man?"

"Sure, make me the bad guy for waking him," he smiles at me.

I notice the cameras on the porch and roll my eyes. "Really? Cameras?"

"They line all the way to your mum's house as well."

"That is a little excessive."

"Nothing is too much when it comes to the safety of our family."

Tears sting my eyes as I walk into our home, to the high ceiling and open top floor, to the sandstone kitchen that overlooks the lake. The wall to floor bookshelf, the large wood heater in the lounge room. "There is another one in our bedroom too," he places our son down to walk. The sleep fading from his eyes and he takes in our giant home.

He rushes for the stairs, "careful Larson," but he just gives me a cheeky grin.

"I made him a giant playroom if you want to start christening areas of our house?"

"It's like you want me to go into labour."

He kneels down and kisses my giant belly; he never has a problem kneeling for me now. "Please do Petal, then I can put another baby in you." He looks up at me with those sea-green eyes.

"I remember saying two children."

He stands, "I didn't build you this many bedrooms to only have two children Petal."

I scoff, "impossible."

"Not with the way I fuck you," he smiles mischievously.

"YOU are impossible," I emphasise.

"Mummy, look!" Larson comes running over with a stuffed teddy.

"Want me to lock him in the playroom?"

"Is it baby proofed?"

"Yes, not a knife or gun in sight." I roll my eyes and smack his arm. "I save those toys for his mother," he whispers against my ear, and the heat creeps along my cheeks.

"I need to show you something first." I hope it is all done, I couldn't be certain because I was under strict orders not to come here.

I lead him out the back where we are greeted with a large lawn area and purple flowers lining the lawn. Trees with dark purple leaves and purple bushes. "So you can always see the happiness," I whisper.

His eyes glass over, "you came here?"

"No, I paid a bunch of gardeners to do this overnight."

Larson picks me a flower, and Atlas bends down to lift him over his shoulders. "I fucking love you, Petal," he whispers against my ear.

My dark-haired boy with green eyes giggles as his dad runs around with him on our lawn. I smile at the life we have created together. Every now and then, Atlas, Bre and Lewis would come on book tours with me, while mum stayed home and watched Larson. Funny thing, once I started having Atlas at my signings, more girls seemed to want my signature. Every once in a while, a crazed stalker would come into my life, but they always seemed to disappear shortly after...

I went through hell before I met Atlas, and then I fell even deeper with him. So lost in his darkness, I thought it would consume me wholly, and it did, of course. Once I saw his darkness as true freedom, as a kingdom in which I rule, then I saw the light.

Then I saw that we are endless.

CONTENT WARNING

- **Murder.**

- **Torture.**

- **Knife play.**

- **Blood and gore.**

- **Dub-con.**

- **Explicit violence, sexual scenes and language.**

- **Choking.**

- **Anal.**

- **Spitting.**

- **Trauma for both main characters.**

- **Breeding kink**

- **Blood play.**

- **Branding.**

- **Gun play.**

- **Orgasm denial.**

ACKNOWLEDGEMENTS

My biggest thank you goes out to my sister Ellen. The person who has spent years supporting and encouraging me, the person who has been my cheerleader even when I felt like giving up. Thank you for all the late-night talks, the research, the guidance and for being my personal assistant. This story would not have made it anywhere without you.

To Mum and Dad, (who can never read this story) thank you for raising me with the confidence to always go after my passions, and for always holding my hand when life gets tough.

To my husband Riley, there are not enough pages to fill all the words I want to write for you. Thank you for being my real-life book boyfriend. For supporting this dream, for being my greatest love and inspiration.

To my brother-in-law Thomas, the first night I had this idea, you spent it quietly researching towns and statistics for me; while we tried not to laugh as the children slept. Thank you for always making me laugh, even in the dark times.

To Emma, for fixing all my many mistakes. For being the editor to my dyslexic brain. You took on becoming a part of my team without hesitation, and your help means the world to me.

To my writer soul mate L.A.Cannon, thank you for always believing in me, for helping and guiding me in this dream. Although our souls have already met, I can't wait for the day we travel across seas to laugh together in real life.

To all my wonderful readers, I will never be able to truly express how grateful I am to you all. Every person that falls in love with my stories is a connection we will have forever. I love you all. Thank you endlessly.

ABOUT THE AUTHOR

Michelle is an Australian writer, who grew up in a small country town. She has spent most of her life working on a farm with her family, but her passion to write has always pulled at her. When she is not busy working and writing, you will find Michelle surrounded by her animals, spending time with friends or family. Taking scenic walks with her husband, or cuddled up watching a new movie or series.

www.ingramcontent.com/pod-product-compliance
Lightning Source LLC
Chambersburg PA
CBHW031950170626
46807CB00006B/2427